THE STORY OF HAGGY BAGGY

A WOMAN'S JOURNEY TO COPE WITH THE LOSS OF HER MISSING DAUGHTER

LIBBE LEAH

Cover and Inside Art and Design by Allyson T. Woolf
Edited by Allyson T. Woolf

ISBN: 1-62436-015-7
ISBN-13: 978-1-62436-015-2

Reel Culture Press, Los Angeles
www.reelculturepress.com

More and more children go missing every year.

Parents—pay close attention to the signs.

Never think for a moment that it can't happen to you.

This story is fiction, but based on reality.

CONTENTS

THE STORY OF HAGGY BAGGY

A WOMAN'S JOURNEY TO COPE WITH THE LOSS OF HER MISSING DAUGHTER

CHAPTER 1

SILENT WARNING SIGNS

Something was in the air. Hagatha Baggard had butterflies in her stomach throughout the morning and afternoon. There was no apparent reason for her to feel that way. She was a healthy and happy-go-lucky fifth grade teacher. She worked at the Robert Lewis Elementary and Middle School in the small town of Emerson, about ten miles south of Boston. Mind you, there were many who would say that being a fifth grade teacher was enough to give anyone butterflies in their stomach, or even an ulcer for that matter—but these today were silent signs, like a warning. It was well known by most teachers that teaching grades five through nine could be a harrowing experience. This was due to all those bouncing hormones, which would continuously bop off the walls of the interior of the classrooms. They were known to bring on temper tantrums, hormonal crying, and testosterone-heavy confrontations by the students of those grade levels. Hagatha had the patience of a saint; she wore a warm smile while calming all her students down.

The school where Hagatha taught was an old stone building with unique carvings of figures along the perimeter of the copper-trimmed roof. It was a storybook setting with the greenest of grass, and the longest ivy vines with pink and yellow flowers—as bright as sunshine—climbing the walls. The beautiful flowerbeds were planted and maintained by the kindergarten teachers with their students every spring. They would start at the middle schools and work their way to the junior high and high schools. The five and six year olds loved digging with their chubby little fingers in the warm wet dirt, using one finger to push the individual seeds down into the fertile earth. For the most part, they were pretty quiet. Except for the times when one of the children would dig deep into the earth, and pull up a big worm! This caused an eruption of loud screeches and screams from the girls, and equally loud oohs and aahs from the boys. The squealing would continue until the teacher bravely marched over and rescued the fat worm from the chubby fingers of the child holding it. Then she would gently place it back into the dirt, being sure to cover it with more dirt, so that the children didn't pull it from the safety of its warm home once again.

Hagatha was forty-two years old, and had been a teacher for twenty years. She loved her life and was devoted to her job. On her own time, she went to each school to help out with extra projects. Her work was within walking distance of her home, just a twenty-minute walk each way. Not only did she find her walks to and from school relaxing, she also always reminded herself that it was great exercise. Hagatha didn't want the added inches on her hips that so many of her co-workers seemed to carry as they too hit their forties. She explained to her husband Marcel, "I don't want to buy new clothes every year. I have to maintain my weight to save our hard-earned money for Clover." "Yes, dear, whatever you say," he would tell her. He never cared if she had a few extra pounds on her. He'd laugh and say, "The more the merrier."

Her reputation as a smart, high-spirited, and energetic woman was well earned in the town where she lived. More than that, she was known for her talent at inspiring young people to learn. Hagatha was extremely creative and positive. It was these two traits that were her tools to inspire students. She was a multi-tasking teacher. Her art, gardening, and furniture crafting were amazing. She gave her students hands-on experience, whether it was in the classroom, on a field trip, or having an early Fourth of July or Halloween Party.

One year, Hagatha had her class design a haunted house for the school. She allowed the children to create the haunted house right in the barn in her yard. The children were very creative, with ghosts that jumped out and grabbed people, and flying witches that cackled loudly and flew out of nowhere only to disappear into thin air. Then there was the

"Feeling Room." In this room, in huge bowls, a variety of wet, moist, animated, textured brews had been concocted, and when they came to visit the room, all the children had to wear a blindfold and put their hands into the different bowls. There were squeals, screams, yells, and groans galore. But the children thought the funniest thing of all was when the school principal visited. Someone dropped a live frog into the large tapioca eyeball bowl. The principal stuck his hand in and the frog leaped onto the back of his hand, making him scream out loud. The children giggled and roared with laughter; they belly laughed so hard that they all had sore stomachs afterwards. This, thanks to Hagatha and her students, went down in history as the best Halloween that Robert Lewis Elementary School had ever celebrated.

The townspeople were familiar with Hagatha for having a generous heart and always helping others in need. Every Christmas, Hagatha and her fifteen-year-old daughter, Clover, would go from house to house gathering warm clothes for the poor, and at least one present from each family for children whose holiday otherwise would be bleak. Hagatha and Clover also helped at the center for unwed mothers, bringing the young women body lotion and other small luxuries. Sometimes Clover would make lists of boys' and girls' names to help the women decide what to call their soon-to-be-born babies. Hagatha and Clover happily refurbished their worn-out jeans, sewing on new buttons and patches that embellished them with the flair of designer wear. Clover loved to sew for the expectant mothers and also painted pictures of plants and clover on their maternity tops that so impressed the women that they wanted to learn how to paint and sew too. She promised that this coming summer she would do arts and crafts with them to see who might be able to get jobs in those fields. The staff at the home urged Clover to show her designs to small boutiques.

During the school week, Hagatha made brown bag lunches for Clover and herself. Not so for Mr. Baggard, who enjoyed taking clients to restaurants or eating out solo. Today, Hagatha didn't have any appetite and barely touched her sandwich, an unusual occurrence for her. The teacher sitting across from her in the lounge kidded with her, saying, "Well, maybe you're pregnant and you don't know it." She shook her head . . . no.

Hagatha was queasy, but pregnancy was out of the question and she jokingly responded with, "Yes, as pregnant as Mother Theresa. I've tried for many years and nothing's happened. I can't be pregnant, that's out of the question. Maybe I'm experiencing early signs of menopause?" Hagatha paused for a moment. "Unfortunately, this doesn't feel like I'm having a child. It feels as though my body is trying to tell me something and I don't know the reason why. It's not like me to feel nervous."

Her co-worker responded with, "Well then, maybe you're going through the change. Have you had any hot or cold flashes?" Hagatha considered that for a brief moment, but then realized that her co-worker simply liked to talk a lot. She replied, "Only when I open my oven when it's turned on, or get something out of the freezer, do I have a flash—a noticeable one. I immediately look for a fan." Hagatha grinned at her friend, and they both burst into laughter. Just then the end of recess bell rang, and they both rushed off to their classrooms. "How silly am I?" thought Hagatha. "I can't be starting menopause yet."

Mrs. Baggard was particularly loved by the children in her class and, of course, by her family. Her distinguished-looking husband, Marcel, loved his wife, and their beautiful daughter Clover, who was picture perfect, adored her mom. Clover had big, brown eyes just like a puppy dog. Her smile was wide and sincere, charming everyone she met. Clover was always filled with laughter and found humor in the most extraordinary things. There were many times when Hagatha was cooking in the kitchen or cleaning the house and she would hear a burst of laughter from wherever Clover was busy being creative—she was always so inspired to create something. Those were her "happy times."

Clover and her mother had a special relationship. They were as close as two peas in a pod. Hagatha appeared almost as youthful as her daughter and was often mistaken for Clover's sister, especially when they traveled. Whenever this happened, Clover would play along and with a giggle say, "Why yes, this is my big sister Haggy. She's teaching me how to become a fashion designer and one day she and I will have a clothing company in New York City called Haggy Baggy's Repurposed Vintage Clothing." "Shhh," her mother would tell her. "Don't make up stories!" Everyone would ask them if they had a business card yet and Clover would put one hand in her bag and say, "Sorry, I completely forgot them— next time!"

The person assuming they were sisters would always politely say that they couldn't wait to get more information about their up-and-coming business. They assumed it would become very famous since it was going to be located in New York City and would have a big website. It always ended with the person wishing them continued success in their haute couture line. Clover would get the biggest kick out of her fantasy, always telling her mom, "It's going to come true. I promise, Mom!" Okay, Clov," Hagatha would say, "I believe you . . . " Both Clover and Hagatha would erupt into laughter. Then Hagatha would pause to remember she was the mother, and she shouldn't be encouraging her child to tell tall tales. Hagatha would say, "Clover, now you stop that, you know it's not right to go on flights of fancy with strangers just because they don't know you well enough to know you're making up stories." Clover always apologized, "Sorry, Mom, I was just having fun." But as soon as her mother would turn her back, Clover would giggle quietly to herself over the great joke that she and her mother had shared.

During the summer, whenever Marcel was away

on a business trip, Hagatha and Clover would take off in the car, driving long distances on winding back roads in Maine. They'd stop at antique stores, second hand shops, and dog shelters when they could find them. They enjoyed eating at small mom and pop style restaurants with old-fashioned storefronts, almost as if time was turned back to the 1940's. Clover would always be on the lookout for a place that sold its own homemade ice cream. She made sure to get her favorite pistachio ice cream, with two scoops and chocolate sprinkles on the top. Hagatha and Clover behaved like the best of friends, laughing and playing jokes on one another, not the mother and daughter they really were. Their connection was cosmic.

One time while they were exploring a second-hand shop, Clover slipped away from her mother for a few moments. She found some vintage clothing, and a hat that came low over her face and had a dark veil attached. Clover ducked into the changing room at the back of the store. She quickly changed into the vintage clothing, donned the hat, and lowered the black veil over her face. Then she snuck out of the dressing room, and hid behind clothing displays so that her mother couldn't see her. Finally, she found an open spot that had an elevated stage, with a mannequin on it. She stepped up next to the mannequin and posed beside it.

By this time, her mother was frantically—and unsuccessfully—looking all over the store for her. Hagatha was beginning to panic. She walked around more than once, calling Clover's name. Finally, she stopped with her back to the stage that Clover was posing on.

Suddenly, Hagatha heard Clover's voice say softly, "Turn around Mother, I'm right over here."

Hagatha spun around, but still didn't know where Clover's voice had come from. She stood there staring at the mannequins and the clothing racks around them. All of a sudden the mannequin in front of her jumped off the stage and lifted the black veil from its face. Hagatha was so shocked that she let out an ear-piercing scream! The sales lady came over in a panic, "Is everyone all right?" "Yes, yes," Hagatha whispered. "No problem, just let me know if I can help out . . . " said the sales lady, backing away.

Clover laughed out loud, "Mom, I'm sorry—I just couldn't help myself! How do you think I look?" "Great, actually," Hagatha replied, "almost like you were made for that era." Hagatha's heart was beating so hard, she thought it was going to jump right out of her chest. She took a couple of calming breaths before responding further to Clover's prank. "Clover, you scared me half to death! First, I thought I'd lost you in here among all these antiques, and then you jump out of nowhere and scare the heck out of me, and the sales lady too."

"Sorry for scaring you so badly, but I just thought you'd get a laugh out of me dressed as a mannequin; and you didn't even recognize me!" said Clover, grinning from ear to ear as she started to giggle because she'd fooled her mother so well. After a moment or two, Hagatha started to laugh herself. "I can only imagine the funny look I must have had on my face when you jumped down from that stage." This got Clover giggling again, and before long, the two of them were laughing so loudly as they left the store without making a single purchase that the saleslady was beginning to look at them funny.

Hagatha's profession was teaching, but she also had an equally consuming passion for making arts and crafts in the barn at her house. She often assigned art projects to her students to check out their skills. Her drawing skills were remarkable, as were Clover's. They had a Facebook page for posting their latest artistic creations for their friends and family only. Hagatha would often drive miles to search for the unacknowledged treasures others might consider trash: old frames and furniture that she could refurbish and paint with unusual designs. She nicknamed these projects R.R.R.: reclaimed, rehabbed, and reconditioned.

Clover sanded the old tables and chairs to make them smooth and look like new again, while Hagatha transformed them into beautiful, colorful, and eye-catching pieces with her amazing painting skills. Clover would even use old clothes to dress the chairs and tables, pulling the material so that it hugged the furniture's body, and then embellishing them with bows and ribbons and old upholstery tacks. She became quite the upholsterer, using professional upholsterers' material to stuff the chairs. Hagatha was so proud of her daughter. And her husband, ever the businessman, appreciated the artistry, craftsmanship, and work ethic of Hagatha and Clover—his two special girls.

Marcel, who hailed from France and still had his heavy French accent, would tell his wife, "You should try opening a shop, maybe in our barn. It's certainly big enough, although you've bought enough to fill two barns!" "Ha! Ha! You certainly are funny," she retorted, grinning widely at him because she couldn't deny it, they probably could fill two barns with all of their recycled treasures.

At first, Hagatha didn't take Marcel's suggestions seriously. She would bristle each time he mentioned the number of collectibles she owned. "Dear," she would say, "it only seems as though there are too many pieces because they're on display in the house, not in an open space like a shop or a barn, where they would literally fly out the door."

"Well then, as I've said, sell from here, from the barn," Marcel responded, further irritating Hagatha. "And it would be nice to sell your creative items, your old furniture and bric-a-brac, don't you think so, dear?"

Hagatha dismissed his comment with a wave of her hand.

Marcel didn't stop and would continue to try to persuade his wife to open a business. "You'd be as successful as you are at teaching, probably even more so because of your passionate interest in art. Look at our daughter, always decorating something just like you, and she's very talented. Even your mother did it, but she never pursued any career or sold any of the things she created." "You may be right," Hagatha confessed. Grinning, she thought back to Clover's very first art piece, when she glued sequins all over the toilet seat and then professed to them that it was her masterpiece. They left the glitter on the seat as long as comfort would permit, and that was short-lived!

When Marcel took his wife and daughter to visit his homeland in France, he introduced Hagatha to the French version of the shabby chic furniture she loved so much. The furniture there was on a grand scale, not like the simple stuff in the States. "We can convert the old barn into a showroom for all your work, and others' work as well." Marcel told her, "You could use the social media outlets at school and post your artwork the way a gallery would, with email access only, not using your actual names, just pseudonyms. After all, we don't want strangers at our door. Does that sound okay to you?"

"Yes, dear," Hagatha replied, "both Clover and I know how protective you are of us."

Marcel explained further, "That way you could post the name of the store instead, like an online store. Just the town would know you're located here. Word of mouth will spread the news about the store. It's a safe and sufficient strategy. We should avoid large ads."

"But Marcel, how will people know to shop at the barn?" Hagatha asked. "We could do it on a small town scale to begin," he replied. "We could posts ads in all the local groceries, the town hall, schools, and function halls. That should bring in plenty of business. We don't need to be greedy. It'll be fun and we'll have more to add to our savings. Remember, we have no rent at the barn so that saves money there—and all these things will get sold!"

Clover came bursting in with her opinion, "Yeah, Mom, it would be fun running a business. We have so many followers on our Facebook page already. And then my storytelling will be true." Her enthusiasm for the project was boundless. "Do it, Mom, do it!" she repeated. "Customers would know to go to the barn store, not our house. Dad could put a number on the barn door so that number would be different from the house's number. Okay?"

"Come on, really . . . " Hagatha said with a bit of reluctance. Then, "Okay, dear, I give in!" Every member of the Baggard family was on the same page; opening the barn store was a goal they would work toward together. They all hugged to seal the unity of their new venture!

Clover always received A's in school and extra credits in art class. "Clover, you're one of my most talented students," her teacher would say. "You will excel if you continue to pursue art as you grow older." Hagatha agreed with Clover's art teacher. "We should go to art shows and galleries more often," she suggested. The idea of visiting artists' studios excited Clover. "Oh Mom, I can't wait! I want to go to New York and California to see fashion shows. I'm going to go, you wait and see."

"Yes, dear, I know you will, but not right this moment. You'll have to wait until you graduate. In the meantime, we can go to local fashion shows," Hagatha responded.

Clover honed her decorating talent by watching her mother and thumbing through crafts and home decorating magazines. She voraciously read the piles of European decorating books that her mother collected from other teachers who had traveled abroad. Clover would also sift through all the waiting room magazines at her dentist's office until she found the ones devoted to decorating. She would sit mulling over the photos and the possibilities. The receptionist once told Hagatha to take the magazines she wanted home to her daughter. Even when Clover danced—yet another of her interests—she was engaged in the pursuit of artistry.

Hagatha thought hard about the names she could give to her store. Shaking her head, she finally said, "I can't come up with anything. I'm drawing a blank."

"I've got it!" Clover shouted with boisterous excitement.

"Okay," Hagatha said, "what is it?"

With eyes lit up, Clover replied, "We'll call it 'Haggy B's'! Granny always calls you Haggy for short. It's catchy, and I already told you I loved that name for our made-up store. I can answer the phones and say, 'Good morning, Haggy B's, Clover speaking.' " Hagatha tilted her head. "Hmm," she said.

"It's great, I love it!" Hagatha agreed, "Haggy B's it is!" She paused for a moment. "How about Clover's Patch or Clover's Barn instead?"

"No, Mom, it doesn't have a ring to it and this is *your* work and *you* should be the theme. It's *you!* Please?"

Hagatha dashed over to Clover to give her a hug and a kiss. She said, "Will do, my precious one, will do."

Clover then pleaded with her mother to allow her to work alongside her in the store after school. "What do you think, is it a definite yes? Can I work in the store? Please! Dad said he would design and build it and we could decorate. Okay?" Hagatha looked into Clover's eyes, declaring, "Yes, yes you can," with a broad smile across her face. "But you have to keep at least one of your extra-curricular activities going as well. You can't give up both dance and after-school art. Choose one, okay?"

"Okay, Mom. I promise," Clover stated with strong commitment in her young voice . . . then twirled like a ballerina.

Hagatha and Clover vowed to make it happen, sealing their pact with another huge hug. After that, Clover would sit on her bedroom floor night after night amid a mountain of buttons and bows. Sam, her stuffed dog, lay on the bed as if he were watching her. When Clover was younger Hagatha would sometimes catch her talking to Sam as if he were real. As she grew older, she didn't talk to Sam nearly as much as she did in the past—she wanted a real dog so badly.

Haggy B's would not open for another two years. All the family's spare time was spent on building the old barn store. There were many starts and stops as the barn was transformed into a French-style store, but finally it was finished. Clover filled notebooks with her own designs, comparing them to the photographs she cut out of the magazines. She would stand at her mirror like she was getting interviewed: *"So, Miss Clover, are these your latest fashions?"* *"Oh yes,"* she would reply to her imaginary reporter, *"we will be showing those at our next fashion show."*

Marcel's mother sent French decorating books to Hagatha and Clover to peruse for new ideas from the latest Parisian styles. Clover put her color and clothing design strengths to use in a more creative way now. She also added some odd touches to chairs and tables. Clover and her mother collected all styles of furniture to fix and paint: English cottage styles, French, and traditional—but never boring.

Clover's best friend, Loralee, showed an interest in the venture. She started doing her own research on furniture on her computer after school. Loralee even helped by promoting the new store with social media to the locals, taking advantage of school e-mails, and friends and family. Everyone in Emerson replied to the emails, inquiring about the store, and friends in other surrounding small towns responded as well. They were nearly done. They had been working so hard that their own clothes were worn out from all the sanding and painting, and torn from lugging the furniture around. Clover's father would look at their paint speckled faces and clothes and laugh, saying, "My two lady painters and designers!"

Marcel constructed an amazingly beautiful showroom in the barn, and both the interior and exterior looked like a European cottage barn. There were separate areas for large and small furnishings, and a spacious loft with a stairway that had the hefty posts and rails that Clover loved so.

Finally, they were ready for business. The old barn store opened without much fanfare. Everything was in its place; the barn was picture perfect, it was so beautiful. Husband, wife, and daughter admired their work as they stood in the entryway with the opened double doors. The sweet aroma of eucalyptus wafted in the air as the soft winds carried it like magic. There was another section of the barn, a sachet room with one purple wall where freshly grown lavender created a different atmosphere and tables were covered with white cotton embroidered cloths. Distinctive furniture and crafts with redone used clothing that gave the impression of high fashion were on display throughout the store. "This is our barn, Mom, isn't it so beautiful?" "Yes Clover dear, it is—very beautiful!" she answered.

Customers began to visit the barn; a few in the beginning, followed by a deluge of people. Neighbors were so impressed by the restored barn and amazing interior that at the town meeting one of the members suggested that Hagatha take photographs and send them to a magazine. Wanting to be helpful, other neighbors posted it live on Twitter and Facebook without the Baggards' knowledge, generating a lot of online hits.

Hagatha, who could be unassuming at times, protested, saying, "Oh no, I don't want to do that!" Marcel agreed with his wife; they both wanted to start small.

"It's no problem," one of the neighbors said, "it's easy to do. We want everyone to see your lovely barn store. The information is already out there and you can only benefit from the exposure." "Yes," replied the Baggards, "but we'd like to keep it our town's best-kept secret." "I'm sorry. We meant no harm," the well-meaning neighbor explained. "We won't overdo it, don't worry. We understand." The Baggards assumed that all was well—there wouldn't be large ads anymore. "Thanks so much for understanding our point of view," Marcel told them. Nonetheless, lots of online chatting continued.

The Baggards were appreciative of the compliments they received and grateful to their neighbors for the interest they took in the barn, but they didn't want to go overboard with too much exposure. They wanted their store to be a hidden gem, whereabouts unknown except to neighbors and friends. That would give them greater peace of mind. They decided to wait to send photos to a magazine, and to post clothing designs on Clover's Facebook page without Clover posing as a model.

Marcel told Hagatha that the neighbors kept posting anyway despite what they said, but they just did compliments—no personal photos. Although she was usually extroverted, Hagatha didn't like being photographed and she didn't want Clover's photo being widely publicized on the internet. The local media were taking notice of Haggy B's. Clover begged and pleaded with her parents and they relented, allowing her to take her mother's place when the publicity shots for the barn were taken. "Just one shot," they stipulated. "I can do it for you," Clover told her mother, "and my friends will share on my personal Facebook page so other schools will see." Marcel and Hagatha gave in somewhat, saying, "Yes, Clover, we know that, but you're only allowed to post your designs on Facebook, not photos of yourself. That's firm!" "But Mom, I think my friends already posted them and we can't take them off." "Well, *no more*," Hagatha declared. "Is that clear?" "Yes, Mom. Yes, Dad," Clover replied. Marcel took the picture of Clover in profile, wearing a wide smile and her work coveralls, which were splashed in an abstract design of multi-colored paint studded with trinkets. Clover held up a few small items in her hands and the camera clicked and clicked again. The photographs were taken and sent out showing lots of items, without Clover's face.

Sunshine beamed inside the barn and bounced off several mirrors, some of which hung on the wall while others leaned against posts. What a sight it was to see their ideas turn into reality. The Baggard family was tremendously pleased and money poured in. Clover was overwhelmed by happiness and leapt in the air like a ballet dancer. It was all happening on the cusp of her sixteenth birthday. She was so excited that she ran spontaneously back and forth from her mother and father hugging and kissing them. "See, Mom, I told you dreams come true!" "Yes dear, you did," Hagatha said, "but no more fairy tales!" Clover was infused with energy, feeling confident and self-reliant.

"Now, all we need is a dog to make our family complete," stated Clover. "What do you say?" she questioned her parents, smiling widely and hoping they would finally agree. Both Hagatha and Marcel laughed and said, "Maybe after the holidays we'll consider it."

Clover's wide smile slid down her face as her happiness disappeared. "Yeah, sure," she sarcastically replied. Clover no more believed that statement than she believed in Santa Claus, or the Tooth Fairy and the Easter Bunny anymore. She hung her head in disappointment and now didn't believe she would ever get a dog.

Hagatha decided to hire one of her friends, Justine, a substitute teacher who worked part-time teaching reading classes, to help out with the store. Justine was also artistic, doing crafts and making jewelry. Hagatha was such a fan of Justine's jewelry that she bought an old oak and glass jewelry case one day. Marcel picked it up and brought it to the barn especially for Justine to show her exquisite handmade work. Clover lined the three shelves with rich purple velvet to accentuate Justine's pieces.

Hagatha and Clover were planning a festive Christmas celebration event for the store that would take place once school was out for vacation. Everything was coming together, even better than they expected. The locals knew about Haggy B's and the Facebook page had ample friends and followers from town, and now an entire page of the town's newspaper, the *Emerson Beacon*, was going to be devoted to the official grand opening of Haggy B's before Christmas. It would show samples of antiques and furniture arrangements with the photograph of Clover in her painted overalls that Marcel had taken to display her clothing designs for the local buyers.

Clover and Hagatha were preoccupied with selecting which antiques and clothing they would ask the newspaper's photographer to shoot. Hagatha occasionally would become overly enthusiastic about the success of Haggy B's and talked about the possibility of expanding the store. Marcel pulled her back to reality saying, "Whoa, we just opened our doors—slow down!"

"It's not wise to grow too fast in the beginning," Marcel cautioned his wife. "This is our home-based business. Let's wait until we've been in business for a couple of years. After all, we're not looking to become the next Walmart," he said sarcastically. "We want to keep it small: intimate and warm, homey and friendly."

"Okay, you're the boss . . . sometimes," Hagatha joked, "and you are so right!" She smiled and said, "Never did I ever think I would hear those words coming out of my successful businessman husband, I think you may have mellowed some. You would normally be talking about sales margins, quarterly profits, and expansion opportunities." "Yes, yes dear," he answered, "but this is different."

Marcel grinned back at Hagatha and said, "I think I might have to agree with you, maybe I have mellowed some." He took her into his arms and gave her a tight hug. "Oh, how I love you and our daughter—what did I do before you both came into my life?" Hagatha kissed Marcel, then joked, "Well, absolutely nothing of course!"

"Ultimately," Marcel teased, "you're the boss. The store will be part of your retirement plan."

"Retirement? I don't think I want to retire at all. Well, I hope not for a long time to come," Hagatha joked along, smiling and laughing. "Forty-something is the 'in' age to be right now, and seventy-something is when most people retire, even later."

Clover was turning sixteen at the same time as the store was taking off. Life for the Baggards was movie perfect. This year's birthday would be celebrated in an even more memorable way than usual. Every year the Baggards invited relatives from all parts of Massachusetts, other states, and even abroad, to their yearly Christmas party. Because Clover's sixteenth birthday was on December fifteenth, the barn's official opening would coincide with her birthday.

Clover once again began hinting about what it might be like to have a dog. She couldn't control herself despite all the letdowns. She called her parents into the room whenever there was a commercial that had to do with dogs, and she would point out the breeds she liked when the Westminster Dog Show was on TV. One of her favorites was the Sussex spaniel, another was the all-black Cocker Spaniel—but a rescue that looks like them would work just fine!

She would say, "I want a male dog. I plan to name him Sammy. You know, after old, faithful, stuffed Sammy," waving the well-used toy in the air to emphasize her point. "We have to adopt a dog from the rescue center, one that desperately needs a home. He'd be my buddy! I just hope he doesn't poop too much. I'm not crazy about cleaning up dog poop, but if it means I can finally have a real Sammy, it'll be worth it." She explained it all to her parents in great detail. When she got to the poop part though, there wasn't a straight face in the room and they all broke into laughter after her poop comments.

In Clover's imagination, she envisioned Sam right beside her and her mother working in the store. "The barn needs a dog to make it complete," she said.

She went on to explain to her mother. "He'll be a help to us," she said trying to convince her mother, "I'll teach him how to sit, lie down, fetch the mail, and not to sniff our customers when they come to visit. Oh, and he could pull a wagon too, so when our they're finished shopping, we could load up his wagon and he could deliver what they bought to their cars."

"Well of course you will, dear," Hagatha said, trying hard not to laugh after that long and humorous list of tasks the dog should be able to do. She thought the time was right for Clover to have a dog; after all, Clover had been asking for one since she was five years old. Marcel and Hagatha knew it was time, but didn't share that with Clover. They envisioned the best birthday yet for Clover, a "sweet" sixteenth birthday with the only gift the one that she had been anticipating all her life.

Clover was excited, and what a great Christmas season this would be! She loved the barn, and on many evenings would meet Loralee there to do homework. The excitement she felt spilled over from home to school, and all she spoke about was her party and the possibility of receiving a surprise present. She wanted desperately for a puppy to be on its way to her this year even if in her heart she knew she wouldn't be getting one. She still had her dreams.

"Maybe on my birthday," she told her friends. "Or maybe this Christmas."

Loralee was equally hopeful and felt the same joy as Clover. Against her parents' wishes, Clover secretly posted pictures of herself with her stuffed dog Sammy, and of puppies she thought looked like him, on Facebook and Twitter. All her friends said they'd make a wish for her.

Anticipating that many people would see their advertisement in addition to the neighbors' word-of-mouth passing through the surrounding towns like wildfire, the Baggards were preparing themselves for a busy holiday season. Clover's parents discussed celebrating her birthday in a small way with her best friends on the exact day of her birthday, then on Christmas Day inviting all her friends for a grander celebration.

Clover loved the idea. "I can see it now," she said out loud to herself, "a new store, maybe a new dog—wishful thinking—and a slammin' Sweet Sixteen Birthday Party, all celebrated on the holiday!" She would be one happy girl. Clover dreamed about her birthday, writing in her diary about all her teenage hopes, dreams, and wishes.

Clover's maternal grandparents, David and Maura, were anxious to see her and had packed their old video camera; ready to roll the moment they arrived. They were anxious to see her knowing that Hagatha and Marcel planned to give her a puppy this year at last. Happiness filled every inch of the Baggards' home.

Maura was overcome with joy for her daughter and granddaughter's new business. She told Clover that she would make some special angels to sell and the sale money could help her get more vintage clothes to work on. Marcel's mom and dad sent Clover a sterling silver charm bracelet for her birthday for good luck, with clovers, hearts, angels, and a dog charm. All the charms were collected at various antique stores in France.

Clover was so inspired every day that she designed and began sewing her own line of clothing just months before her birthday. Her friends begged her to design and make clothes for them, and it occurred to Hagatha that Clover might well be a designer one day.

Clover and Loralee collected old clothes from their neighbors, who got them from their grandparents or parents, for Clover to remake into her own designs. Hagatha watched her work on a shirt with patches of material and buttons, taking sleeves from a perfectly good shirt and replacing the sleeves of an old, damaged shirt with new unmatched patterns, adding the pattern of the shirt's collar to the mismatching pockets, and attaching dangling chains with trinkets to the front of the shirt that could be used as jewelry. Clover was a true artist, unhampered by conventional thinking.

She would post her designer shirts and jeans on her new web page that she and Loralee were working on. Her work was eclectic, but in the most novel and interesting of ways, her viewers thought.

Two of Clover's favorite designers were Juicy Couture and Betsey Johnson because of their dangling charms and girly-girl look. Loralee designed a web page featuring Clover's creations: Clover's Recycled and Redesigned. Disorganized at first, she made a few false starts. Self-taught, she caught on and posted the clothes in an unconventional, funky—though organized—way using her dad's and grandfather's antique cameras, an old desk, and hat boxes. She even took the pictures in the unfinished angled attic space her mom used just for storage.

When Clover saw Loralee's handiwork on the website, she whooped with joy. She grabbed one of the feather boas that Loralee had tossed around her room. Then Clover wrapped it around her neck in a dramatic way, put on a pair of Loralee's fluorescent pink sunglasses, and began to dance around the room.

"I can see it now Loralee, when we grow up, I'll be a famous fashion designer like Betsey Johnson and you'll be my manager and publicist!" Clover shouted out loud, her face glowing with excitement. Both girls looked at each other and jumped up and down and screamed in anticipation. Loralee put an oldie but a goodie on her MP3 player—"Girls Just Want To Have Fun"—and both Clover and Loralee, wrapped in feather boas and their funky running shoes, danced around the room, while the recorded voice of Cindy Lauper echoed off the walls.

Meanwhile, back at home, Hagatha was on the same track as her daughter. She asked Marcel about what he foresaw for Clover's future, and he replied, "If designing is what she wants and it makes her happy, then that's what she should do." Every one of Clover's teachers, as well as her whole family, knew that she would follow a design career rather than go to a business college, and her parents would use the money they had saved for a top design school and trips to study abroad. Clover, of course, insisted on being in Paris or Madrid. Marcel assured Hagatha that with all their income they would have more than enough by the time Clover graduated high school. He said, "If Clover actually goes to Paris, she could live with my parents or stay with her Aunt Antoinette, then on to Madrid in a couple of years." Aunt Antoinette had a son and daughter close to Clover's age, and they had friends in Madrid she could stay with when she went there. "Don't worry, Hagatha, our baby girl will be in good hands when she travels to Paris. She'll be surrounded by family that loves her and will take good care of her while she's with them."

"You're right, of course, Marcel. Sometimes I forget that she's almost all grown up, and not just my little baby girl anymore. I wish I could've kept her little forever, but then Clover wouldn't be the vivacious, charismatic, and gifted young woman that she is today. Oh, if I'd been able to do that or took the chance to do it, but I never created those chic, unusual designs like our daughter has. I think I would've missed seeing her coming into her own as she is now had I been a designer and on the road. Sometimes she surprises me at how mature she's become. But every so often she slips back into little girl mode. Did I tell you that when I went to check on her in her room the other day, she was playing dress-up with one of her new funky outfits. Her hair was drawn up into pigtails, with multi-colored ribbons woven through them. But the pièce de résistance was that she'd painted her face to look like a clown, using the same makeup she normally wears only sparingly to school. I found her dressed like that and doing cartwheels in her room. So that child we knew and will always love is not too deep below the surface." Hagatha explained detail after detail to Marcel. Then both she and Marcel burst into laughter at all the wonderful memories that flooded back from Clover's childhood.

Clover renamed her line of clothing again, calling it " 'Très Jolie' by Clover C.—Making Old New Again." She felt that was a better name than the first one. Taken as she was by the beauty of the cherubs she saw in photographs of Paris, she told her mom she was working on a logo adorned with cherubs.

Despite all the plans Hagatha, Marcel, and Clover made, they could not predict what the future would bring. This year would not only change their lives, it would mark the end of life as they had known it.

CHAPTER 2

THE BAGGARDS

The Baggards' home was a large Colonial house on a slight slope, with many stone steps that led to the front door. Their address was 17 Holly Place; the street was named for the daughter of the builder who constructed all the homes on the street. The back of the majestic house at 17 Holly Place rested on flat land carpeted by green grass and adorned with several gardens of pink peonies, pink hydrangeas, wine-colored perennials, and Hagatha's large pink clover patch that burst into bloom in early spring and summer. The view was like an exquisite postcard. Guests of the Baggards would sometimes enter through the back door of the house just to see the floral arrangements in Hagatha's elaborate cement pots. Hagatha always said it was a shame that the back door wasn't located in the front.

On either side of the front flagstone walkway, Hagatha planted several rows of wild crimson clover and other beautiful wildflowers that gave the front of the house the look of an English garden, with cherub statues that Clover loved. As a child, Clover jumped from stone to stone, improvising her own version of hopscotch. And there it was—the wonderful barn at the back of the house. The path that led to the barn was bordered with pink and white flock flowers, like a passageway in a fairy tale. Marcel's mother, a master gardener, helped Hagatha with her garden decor. Whitewashed benches, with flowered cushions from Paris that Marcel's mother made, were placed along the pathway in the springtime. Often, people driving by or friends of neighbors stopped to take photos of the yard. The Baggards would find notes on their front door, with the name and telephone number of the person who taped the note there, asking for their landscaper's information. Marcel always got a kick out of teasing Hagatha. "Hagatha, I think a change of careers is in order for you. I think we could probably grow Clover's education fund even faster if I hired you out as a landscape architect," he said. Then he grinned broadly at his wife, put his arm around her, and pulled her up against him. "I love you, dear," he said. "And I love you too," Hagatha replied. "We are so blessed."

"Well, landscaping sounds easy—and nice of you to suggest—but how would I get my kid fix every day, unless I hired the entire kindergarten class to help me landscape those yards. But production wouldn't be very good because you know the first one to find the worm would either be screaming or chasing the others with it. So I think I'll keep the job I've got." She smiled back at him and snuggled into his side. Clover often told her mom, "I want to have a husband just like Daddy. You both are so much in love." "You will, my love," Hagatha assured her.

When the colors of the house faded and needed painting, all three of them picked up a brush, with Marcel painting the top, Hagatha the middle, and Clover the bottom around the porches. In the end, the house looked like professional painters had done the job. Hagatha found that painting below her husband made for the effect of wearing bird droppings of paint on her clothes. But poor Clover got it the worst, as she was on the bottom and experienced a rain shower of paint dripping down on her from both her mother and her father's brushes. She was covered with patterns of colored dots on her hair, face, and arms. Hagatha said, "If I didn't know you'd already had chicken pox, I would think you got a very colorful, new chicken pox virus. You are literally covered in colorful spots from the top of your head to the tip of your toes!" Both she and Marcel looked at Clover. Marcel took pictures with his phone while they burst out into belly-rolling laughter.

"Well I guess the upside is I made you laugh, Daddy. The downside is it's going to take forever to get all these dots of paint off me," Clover said as she looked at her reflection in the porch window. "But I think I'll leave the paint dots on my clothes, because they look really artsy and I can wear them, and everyone will want me to make them a pair too." Once again, Hagatha and Marcel cracked up as they watched Clover show her spots off, with the drops of paint on her nose. They could always rely on Clover to find the silver lining in any situation.

Their oversized barn off to the side at the rear of the house not only created a beautiful pastoral scene, but was also quite chic. The old Volkswagen bug Hagatha was saving for Clover when she graduated looked like a vintage car and fit right into the scene.

When Clover was a child she used to play in the barn. She had to ask her daddy to remove the cobwebs so the spiders wouldn't crawl over her or her dolls, and he would always answer, "Anything for my girl! We don't want those spiders on my Clover, do we?" To which she would reply, "No, Daddy we don't." For fun, she would run up and down the winding stairs to the barn's loft, where she would line up her toys in perfect order. Even then, Clover enjoyed dressing and undressing her dolls, constantly switching their outfits and gluing candy dots and old broken jewelry on them. She was a high-spirited child with energy to spare, and loved everything.

Hagatha always had to remind Clover to be careful sliding down the old post. "You could get a splinter," she would tell Clover time and time again.

And every time, Clover replied, "Don't worry, Mom. I'm fine. I like playing up here, and when I slide down I feel like a flying angel!" Hagatha relented in the end. "Well, we can always pull the splinter out if that's the worst that can happen," she thought. "She should have her fun."

Without mentioning it, Marcel sanded and varnished the rail anyway so that there wouldn't be any chance of accidents.

Clover had asked her parents for a dog countless times, saying, "Please, when will I get my very own dog? Please?" She realized that the older she got the less likely it would be for her mom and dad to agree to a dog—the dog would have to stay home with them when she left for college.

"I'll buy myself a dog when I'm out of college," she would say somewhat defiantly. While Clover loved her parents tremendously, she did harbor some resentment about the fact that she had gone her entire childhood without the companionship of a dog, which she wanted desperately. Like all children, she would get that face on when she saw a dog and say, "I'll run away and get a dog, then bring it home so you have to keep it!" "Okay, my little girl," Marcel would reply, "I'll pack you a lunch for your journey . . . and you go get a bone for the dog." As Clover got older she stopped her not-so-subtle threats.

And as for the possibility of that dog arriving— Marcel and Hagatha always said "soon," but "soon" never arrived. Clover sat outside on the wide stairs with a sad face and sometimes Loralee would join her, sharing in her sadness.

Loralee said, "Don't worry, Clov. If I get a dog before you, I'll name it Sammy and it'll belong to both of us, okay?"

"Okay. And I'll do the same," Clover always replied. It was their secret pact, often sealed with a comforting hug. So many birthdays passed by without Clover receiving her long awaited wish. Every Christmas when Clover was younger, she placed a folded note requesting a dog from Santa on the dining room table next to the cookie dish, along with a dog bone she would get from one of her neighbors. Even though she had stopped writing to Santa by the time she was twelve, she still continued pressuring her parents.

She hinted and left them notes on the refrigerator and table saying, "Remember, Mom and Dad, my only wish is for a dog, please?" She collected photographs of various dogs she left around the house.

Loralee, like Clover, was an only child. Loralee asked her parents for a dog to share with Clover. Loralee never asked for a puppy for herself. "Taking care of a pet is a large responsibility," Evelyn, Loralee's mother, said, "and it's something we aren't prepared to do. Wanting a dog for your friend is not a good enough reason to bring a pet into our home."

Loralee understood, but she was disappointed that she couldn't help her friend.

Sometimes, at night, Clover would stare at the stars, asking them and the angels to grant her wish for a puppy. At nearly sixteen, she persisted in writing in her diary about wanting her own dog. She had decided to stop leaving notes on the table and confided in Loralee that she didn't expect a dog this year, or any year for that matter. "I just don't understand my parents," Clover said. "All these years they've been promising me a dog. In two more years, I'll be heading off to college. I just feel betrayed by them. Why promise they'll get me a dog and then never follow through? I think I've been very patient all these years. All I want is a dog to love and cuddle and share things with. Loralee, can't you see you and me and a dog running through our garden trying to catch butterflies, and the dog bouncing behind, barking and playing Frisbee?" she asked Loralee with a look of happiness lighting her face.

Loralee agreed with Clover and said, "Or you could bring him out to the barn and we could teach him how to fetch stuff for us. We could say, 'Just follow that dog and he'll show you our barn store.'" Loralee looked over at Clover and they both burst into laughter at the thought of the dog showing customers around the barn. Then Clover's mind returned to reality.

"It's too late," she said, "it'll never happen and I'm not going to ask anymore. Most likely, my parents think that they'll end up taking care of the dog when I graduate and go off to school somewhere. And I do understand their concerns." That was the end of it. Loralee never got a dog either because, as her mom said, the responsibility was more than they could handle and Loralee confessed that she really didn't want to take care of a dog all by herself. "If Clover and I ever become roommates, then we'll get a dog together," she told her mom.

Everything was good. Everything would continue to be good. Clover and Loralee had their future planned out.

CHAPTER 3

VANISHED

Hagatha and Marcel sat on the steps listening to the blare of sirens in the distance. This was an unusual sound for their small, orderly town and the noise pierced the quiet of the evening. Tomorrow will be Clover's birthday. They knew that she could hardly wait and her parents were just as excited about all their plans. First they would have a small party. Then the grand holiday celebration would take place.

But something utterly terrifying has happened . . . Clover has vanished!

Loralee had walked Clover home as she did every school day. Clover's house was first on their route, and Loralee lived a bit further up the hill at the end of the street in a house well hidden, with a winding driveway that led to a path of tree-lined steps. Clover loved her friend's house—it was spacious and colorful, so untraditional and artsy.

When both girls were twelve years old, their parents decided it would be safer for them if, every day, they walked home from school together rather than alone. The girls were adamant about walking. They said they were too old to be driven. All their friends at school were walking home without any supervision. Hagatha and Evelyn allowed them to walk home together with the stipulation that both of them go straight home before going anywhere else.

Even though they followed their parents' instructions, something had happened to Clover! She hadn't gone directly inside her house after school. There were no signs of her entry. No one knew where she was. Clover had disappeared. Where? Who did she meet? *What went wrong?*

The Emerson police were called.

Clover wasn't there as she normally was when Hagatha arrived home from teaching at three-thirty. Clover never missed a day. Usually, Hagatha found her in the kitchen eating spoonfuls of peanut butter and jelly. But not today. There was no note on the kitchen table and no school bag.

Clover hadn't called to tell anyone where she was going—this wasn't like her at all! Did someone approach her? Did someone pick her up? Was it as simple as her neglecting to tell anyone where she was planning to go? Maybe she went to a friend's house to discuss her ideas for designing a dress or a pair of jeans. But no one knew anything, nothing made sense—nothing!

Loralee told Hagatha when they spoke on the phone that, "She must've forgotten something at school and went back there!" But when Hagatha called the school office she was informed that no one had seen Clover. When it was close to five o' clock and Clover still hadn't come home yet, Hagatha shook and shivered as if a tremendous cold wave had washed over her as she stood at the shoreline. She wanted to leave her house, where she felt so alone. Although she was uncertain about leaving, Loralee had suggested on the phone that Hagatha come over and research rescue centers for dogs with her.

"She wasn't planning to leave a note about a dog this year, Mrs. B.," Loralee said. "Maybe she's checking out the dogs. It is strange, though, that Clover didn't tell me. Then again, she does love secrets."

"Yes, you may be right about the rescues. We can do an online search and call them all," stated Hagatha, with a worried tone in her voice.

"I'll help and call places where she might be," Loralee offered, also deeply worried about her friend.

"Loralee, I really would love to come over but I need to stay here at home to look through Clover's things."

"Okay, Mrs. B., I understand," Loralee replied in a shaky voice.

Hagatha phoned several animal shelters, but no one had seen her. In a panic, she called the school again as well as the student centers. Most of the staff had already gone home and the few remaining teachers and students gave their word to call her if anyone had information about Clover's whereabouts. Hagatha went through her list of teachers' home numbers, including the principal's home phone number, but no one had seen Clover since school let out that afternoon.

Everything was exactly as she had left it in the morning. There wasn't any sign that Clover had been home at all. The house at 17 Holly Place was empty except for Hagatha, who was caught in the grasp of the horror of it all. Troubled, she paced the floor, opening the drawers to the buffet and end tables where Clover might have put a piece of paper with some clue, a friend's phone number—anything!

Painful hours passed. The sky was dark. Hagatha paced the kitchen floor nervously. She tried to ignore the gnawing in her gut that was telling her that something had gone terribly wrong. It was the same strange sensation she had felt since early that morning at school. Being so closely tied to Clover, she actually felt terrified as she experienced a sense of foreboding overcome her.

Hagatha began to sob uncontrollably, asking, "Where is my little girl? I knew something wasn't right all day! I knew I should've gone home early!" The thought of calling Marcel flashed across her mind. She did not want to call him in a panic and decided to put off telling her husband until she had calmed down and was completely certain Clover was missing. Maybe that would give some more time for Clover to appear. She understood that if she waited he'd be upset with her, but she waited nonetheless.

"Come home, Clover," she repeated over and over again.

"There has to be a reasonable explanation," she said out loud, although her mind was plagued with tormenting thoughts. The house phone rang. She was trembling, thinking the call was from Clover or someone else who had found her. Maybe she was hurt! Hagatha rushed to answer it. She tripped over the doorway and fell to her knees. She saw that one of her knees was scraped, red and swelling, but she was numb to any physical pain. A few drops of blood trickled down her shin from the scrape on her knee and she hoisted herself up, leaning against the wall, listening to the constant ringing of the phone.

Breathing heavily she answered the call, "Hello? Hello?" But, no luck—it wasn't Clover, it was her close neighbor and friend, Evelyn. "Oh, Evelyn. Where's my baby?"

Evelyn expressed her concern, "Don't worry, she'll be home soon. Did you call Marcel yet?"

"No. I have to do that as soon as we hang up." "Do you want to come over to my house?" Evelyn asked. "No, not now," Hagatha replied. "Why don't I come over there, then," Evelyn suggested. Hagatha said no, not just yet, thanked her for her concern, and hung up immediately without saying goodbye, not wanting to take the time to speak to her any longer.

Hagatha sobbed, deep-rooted sobs that seemed to come from her very soul. She leaned her back against the wall and stared at the phone's receiver, wishing that the phone would ring again. "Please call, Clover, and tell me where you are, please, please! Clover will be here any minute now. She's a teenager—not a baby—and she'll be home soon. I'm jumping the gun."

She sensed a sinking feeling and then an urgency inside her. She could feel each moment slipping away, taking her further away from her beloved daughter. Sitting on the highest step of the stairway, she hunched over and felt dizzy, but regained her balance reading through the names and numbers in Clover's old phonebook and then her own, studying each name as tears dropped on the pages. Her tears wet the paper and the ink began to slightly smudge on the pages. "Damn . . . damn," she cursed as she patted the papers dry. However, she found nothing unusual.

The front door was open and a frigid wind blew into the foyer. It was cold outside and the house was getting just as cold, but Hagatha didn't care. Her hands shook and a shiver traveled down her spine. Again, she felt the pit in the hollow of her stomach, and now, to add to that, a pain in her heart as if she knew that Clover was in distress and in serious trouble. The pain was palpable, physical, and deep— her heart ached. At first she thought she might be having a heart attack, but after a moment she recognized the feeling. It was fright, heartbreak, and an empty feeling of loss. She recognized the panic from when Clover was a toddler and climbed out of her crib, striking her head on the hard floor. She and

Marcel had rushed her to the emergency room and waited anxiously in the hospital until the doctors said she was fine.

"Oh please, please come home!" she said aloud, leaning forward and clasping her arms around her knees.

Hagatha couldn't tolerate staying at home and waiting any longer. She ran into the kitchen to find her car keys. She left her pocketbook open, sitting in the middle of the kitchen table, and dashed out the door without taking any identification. She let the car idle while she sat for a moment considering where to go first and to calm herself. Perhaps Clover had gone to the library, or the bakery where she might be looking at the colorful frosted birthday cakes in the refrigerated cases. She always stared at the chocolate ones whenever she was there, wanting to eat the rich, dark frosting without the cake.

"Yes, they're still open," she said, as she checked the car clock. "They stay open until 8 p.m. during November and December." Her mind was racing. Hagatha shivered; she'd rushed out of the house without putting on her coat. Before heading to the bakery, she stopped at each house on the street and, in a panicky manner, ran to her neighbors' doors asking if they'd seen Clover. When they said they hadn't seen her, she became even more frantic, running from the lit doorways to her car, pressing hard on the gas pedal and driving erratically.

The dark blue sedan was swerving from one lane to the next when Hagatha noticed how out of control her driving had become. She slowed down. Her heart beat rapidly. Pulling over to the side of the road, she took several deep breaths as she tried to collect herself. Resting her head on the steering wheel, she burst into tears and sobbed uncontrollably until there were no more tears to be shed.

She drove on and stopped in front of the bakery, frantically opened the door, and ran up to the front entrance. The girl behind the counter was busy putting away what would become their day-old products when they opened tomorrow. Hagatha stormed in and pounded loudly on the counter with her fist. The girl looked up and saw a red-faced, frazzled-looking woman, with her hair flying wildly off her face and bloodshot eyes. Seeing the desperation in Hagatha's eyes, the girl came over to the counter immediately and said, "Yes Ma'am, may I help you? Are you all right?"

Hagatha leaned over the counter, looking directly into the young girl's eyes and said, "Do you know Clover Baggard? Please tell me you do!"

The young girl nodded her head and said, "Yes, I know her from school, and she comes in here a lot and gets free samples, but lately she hasn't been coming around. At school she told me she's been dreaming about the birthday cakes we have, and which one she'd most like to have on her birthday. I haven't seen her for a few days."

Hagatha reached over and held the young girl's shoulder tightly, almost to the point of hurting her in her desperation. "Have you seen Clover today at all?" Hagatha questioned loudly in a high-pitched wavering voice.

The girl shook her head no. "I haven't seen her, Ma'am. We're not in the same classes. Is there anything else I can help you with?" Hagatha removed her hands from the girl and drew her arms around her own waist.

"I'm so sorry. Forgive me, please. If you do happen to see her, please call me, or have her call me at home. She's missing. She never came into the house after coming home from school today. So if you hear anything, or talk to anyone who has seen her, please, please call me."

"I'll do that Ma'am. I'm sure she'll be home soon. She might have met up with someone from school."

"Yes, yes. You may be right."

Hagatha nodded and felt like her head was so heavy that it was about to fall off of her neck and roll away across the floor.

"We're closing soon, but I'll talk to everyone I know and ask if they've seen Clover anywhere around town today. Here's a piece of paper to write down your number in case I find out anything." With compassion and sadness clouding over her face, the girl promised to call. Hagatha returned the girl's expression with a sad smile and apologized again for her outlandish behavior.

"My mom would've done the same thing," the girl replied.

Hagatha went to every business in town. She got

out of the car and asked questions, but when she didn't get any of the answers she was hoping for she decided to go back home. Hagatha had to call Marcel. It was far beyond the time when she should have phoned him. She knew she wasn't thinking clearly. The clock was ticking and no one had seen Clover.

Marcel was at a late meeting, which was out of the ordinary for this time of year, but a large conglomerate was interested in acquiring his company and the office was a flurry of activity. Usually the office slowed down in December for the holidays, but not this year.

Hagatha knew that Clover should have called or been home by now. She went back inside the house and noticed her open handbag on the kitchen table. "Oh no," she cried, "I was driving without my license!" Hagatha continued pacing back and forth, limping on the side of her injured leg. She pulled the kitchen drawers wide open and rifled through the contents, looking for telephone numbers on ripped pieces of paper that Clover habitually left scattered about. She found a piece of paper folded in quarters with the phone numbers of some of Clover's new friends and teachers at Emerson. After telephoning them all, it yielded nothing. Their answers were all the same. "No," they said, "we haven't seen Clover since school let out. We're so sorry. We'll watch out and call you if we see or hear something." Hagatha could tell their empathy and concern were genuine, but she would hang up the phone abruptly, too distracted to say goodbye. More calls poured in due to Loralee, who had called all their friends at Emerson, and other schools as well. Hagatha showed little emotion, and then—click—she would hang up the receiver.

Hagatha couldn't wait any longer. Suddenly her husband's meeting didn't seem quite as important as it usually did. She paused, trying to breathe deeply. She picked up the phone and dialed her husband. But when she heard his voice she became overly emotional, barely managing to speak between her pitiful sobs. Hagatha was falling apart.

Marcel attempted to console his wife, saying, "Please calm down and tell me what happened clearly and slowly. I can't understand you. What about Clover?"

Hagatha screamed loudly into the phone, "Clover, our baby, hasn't come home!"

Marcel asked, "From school?"

"Yes, from school," she replied trying to calm herself down.

Marcel responded with, "She's responsible and hasn't gone far, I'm sure. She's an adolescent. This is the first time she hasn't called to let us know where she is. We'll find her. She can't be far. Remember, her birthday is tomorrow so she may have wandered downtown to window shop. Why did you wait so long to call me, Hagatha?"

There was silence at the other end of the receiver. She didn't want to believe her precious daughter was actually missing. She couldn't answer her husband's simple question and faltered, stuttering, "I, I, I . . . "

"Stay put, I'm on my way! Did you call the police yet?"

"No, Marcel, I didn't." Hagatha responded with a desperate tone to her voice.

"Okay! Okay! I'll deal with it when I get home."

Hagatha hadn't called him because she didn't want to upset him. He was annoyed that his wife hadn't called him sooner, but once he arrived home, Marcel quickly grasped the gravity of the situation—CLOVER WAS GONE! There was no trace of her being in the house. No peanut butter and jelly smeared on the kitchen counter or any indication she'd been there at all. He felt a dull pain in his chest. Now the terror fully hit him and he understood Hagatha's panic and hesitation.

She flung herself into his arms. "Clover's a good girl. She'll be home soon, won't she Marcel?" Hagatha believed with all her heart and soul that their daughter would be back. Clover had never strayed before and she would be sixteen, after all, in another day. "I know she's not a baby. Maybe she has a boyfriend that she never told us about," Marcel speculated. "Perhaps she's gone out to meet him somewhere."

"No dear, I doubt that. Clover's pretty open with us about things like that. Anyway, Loralee would know about a boyfriend if she had one. She would've mentioned it when we spoke," Hagatha said, confident that she was right about both her daughter and Loralee.

"Yes, you're exactly right, dear. Loralee would've been the first to tell us if a boy was involved so that we wouldn't worry. At the very least, though, Clover should've left us a note," Marcel replied.

Hagatha agreed, pulling at strands of her hair as she spoke, "I don't understand! There's no trace of her, no indication that she ever came inside!" Marcel cried out in anguish as the gravity of the situation sunk in even further.

"No, no trace, I checked several times." Hagatha stated with a look of fear that had settled upon her face like a mask.

"We have to call the police—now!" Marcel bellowed.

The Emerson police were called. In the small town of about 15,000, the officers were familiar with many of its residents. It was the sound of the sirens Hagatha and Marcel heard while waiting on the steps that confirmed their fears that Clover might be in some sort of danger.

The cruiser arrived and one of the two officers in uniform, Lieutenant Freeman, asked, "Mr. and Mrs. Baggard, would you please explain why you think your daughter may be missing?"

Hagatha explained, and then the lieutenant questioned her about the possibility of Clover having a boyfriend or if she might be at a friend's house. Hagatha was distraught, overwhelmed, and nearing emotional exhaustion. Lieutenant Freeman noted the Baggard's anxiety and asked them to sit down and try to relax while they continued to question them.

Marcel and Hagatha handed them a list of Clover's friends, assuring them that her boyfriends were just friends.

Hagatha's words tripped over each other as she quickly told the police, "Clover and Loralee would go to the movies occasionally with one boy in particular from time to time but in no way were Clover or Loralee romantically involved with him."

"Yes, Mrs. Baggard," the lieutenant said. "Could you please slow down? I want to be clear about everything you say, especially the names of people who may have information about your daughter."

Hagatha explained, "I've already called all the people who had a connection to Clover. Even people remotely connected to her." Hagatha showed them the list of the phone calls that she had made and the time of day she made them. The lieutenant commented on the thoroughness of her work and thanked her.

She was trying her best to hold herself together for Clover's sake, so that she could help the officers find her daughter.

The lieutenant said, "Regardless of your efforts, my officers have to check out everyone. Emotions can sometimes blur our memories so it's best that we recheck your steps. No offense meant to you."

With that in mind and without another word, Hagatha handed them the list, along with phonebooks. Marcel admired his wife because she had organized a list of names and made phone calls amid her confusion and panic. He knew all too well that his wife's silence was an indication of her somber mood.

"We'll be coming back for your daughter's computer if she doesn't return home or isn't found soon," Lieutenant Freeman told Marcel and Hagatha, as they held each other tightly.

Hagatha asked the other officer if he thought Clover was all right.

"Yes Ma'am, I think she'll be fine. Everything will turn out all right," the officer responded confidently.

Hagatha pressed her head against Marcel's shoulder to hide the tears she'd been holding back during Lieutenant Freeman's interview.

As the two policemen started to leave, one officer turned and said, "Don't worry too much. Teenagers are unpredictable." The Baggards breathed a sigh of relief. Both officers left and went door to door to every house in the neighborhood. Neighbors and friends gave whatever information they could. They formed small groups to search for Clover in the expanse of woods behind their homes and wherever else the police asked them to look.

The police provided one of the groups with locations of parking lots where groups of young people were known to congregate after school and into the evening.

Lieutenant Freeman stated, "I still haven't ruled out the possibility of Clover having a secret boyfriend no matter how unlikely it is. And we should spread out to other towns." The lieutenant was just being thorough. He knocked on Loralee's front door, and when she answered Lieutenant Freeman questioned her right off about Clover's whereabouts and whether there was a boy involved in her apparent disappearance. They knew that Loralee was Clover's closest friend and that she was integral to their investigation.

But Loralee took offense to his statement about boyfriends and told the policeman, "I would've known about a boyfriend long before anyone else—I'm her best friend."

"I'm sorry if I've stepped on anyone's toes, but I need to be as direct and straightforward as possible, Miss."

The police had questioned the Baggards about Clover's internet activity, asking, "Was she online a lot and did she visit any teen or chat sites?" They followed the same line of questioning with Loralee and her mom. They corroborated what Marcel told Lieutenant Freeman and the officers. Lieutenant Freeman returned to the Baggards' home. The front door was open to the outside chill. "Hey there," the lieutenant called, "may I come in? There's more we should discuss. We need as much information as possible to get the ball rolling."

"Of course, please come in and sit down," Hagatha said.

Marcel fielded the questions the lieutenant asked. "Our Clover was always so busy being creative, attending dance class, and working on her school work. She was hardly ever online except when she was posting her latest creations to her Facebook page. I don't even know what a chat site or a teen site is. I believe we'd know what they are if Clover had visited them. She would've shared that with us. My daughter wasn't the type of girl who kept secrets from us. We're a very close-knit family," he explained. Loralee had told the police the same story. Marcel broke down in tears, cradling his face in his hands trying to hide the agonized expression on his face. He was always the strong one, but not now as he cried in Hagatha's arms.

"Our daughter is our life! I can't even fathom how something like this could happen to us," he moaned. Marcel cursed the internet and all computers. "Loralee said that Clover got a text just as she was leaving her off at the door. I don't know, she may have met somebody online. There's too much information about her and her friends available for anyone to read, and photographs to see. I pleaded with her not to post pictures. She could've come in contact with . . . with . . . some sort of predator. We pay close attention to what she does, but it's impossible to know every detail."

"Yes sir, we understand, we have children," the lieutenant said.

"She could be missing for any number of reasons not related to the computer," Lieutenant Freeman stated. "I have a teenager of my own." The Baggards were inconsolable and didn't take comfort from the lieutenant's comment; they sat there feeling all alone.

Hagatha watched her husband as he fell apart. She went to get him a glass of water and as he drank she held him close, her arms embracing his body with her head resting on his chest. "She *will* come home. She has school in the morning," Hagatha said. "She'll be at school in the morning. I have to believe that."

The lieutenant responded with, "It's too early in the search to assume that any one thing is responsible for her disappearance. We simply don't know that yet. It usually takes 24 hours for them to come home."

"She could've texted someone or someone may have picked her up."

"Who did she text?"

Ideas and questions bounced between them as fear coursed through husband and wife. "Yes, she's at an age when it's possible she met someone new whom we aren't aware of," Hagatha told the lieutenant, her voice cracking. "Sometimes Clover keeps secrets even from Loralee."

"Anything we should know about, Mrs. Baggard?"

"No . . . her secrets weren't of any consequence. Once she sold a jacket Loralee had her eye on so she didn't tell her about it right away. It was small stuff she hid, nothing major."

"There must be an explanation," Marcel declared in denial, as much to convince himself as to allay his wife's fear. "I have to believe that our Clover is just late coming home."

"Does anything else come to mind, folks? Anything at all?"

"What other reason could there possibly be?"

Hagatha replied. "Perhaps we're overlooking an important clue. The barn, let's look in the barn! Why didn't I think of looking in there before? She may be in there working on her designs up in the loft!" Hagatha suggested frantically. She flew out of the door ahead of Lieutenant Freeman and Marcel, almost tripping over herself to get to the barn, but there was no indication that Clover had been there. When they discovered no sign of her in the barn, Hagatha was crushed. They had searched every inch.

Marcel's disappointment chipped away at his certainty that Clover would be coming home soon. Hagatha and Marcel, the loving couple, stood across from each other and, bewildered, exchanged a worried frown.

"We should thoroughly examine every room of the house one more time." Hagatha stated, already beginning to retrace her steps back to the house.

"Yes, Mrs. Baggard, we'll check the entire house for you again," one officer said. "From the basement to the attic," added Lieutenant Freeman. A circle of police officers and two detectives gathered in the front hallway waiting for their next order.

"We know her better than the police," Marcel told his cousin, who had just called on the house phone as they were stepping inside. "We can help shed some new light on where she may have gone, maybe more than anyone else. We're certainly very familiar with her belongings; we looked to see if anything was out of place or missing and nothing was," Marcel said, speaking to Hagatha and his cousin while the police went on their exhaustive search.

His cousin offered to help look for her. Marcel thanked him, saying that he would call him if Clover hadn't shown up by tomorrow. "The police on the streets have only a photograph to guide them," Marcel told his cousin. One of the officers standing in the doorway interrupted, "The detectives will take care of everything, Mr. Baggard. They've been with the force for years and have experience with these types of cases."

"Really? How many cases of missing children have there been in our town?" Marcel asked, leaving the officer speechless and feeling defensive.

"Mr. Baggard, I don't know the actual number, but I guess it's in the neighborhood of about five or six over the past fifteen years or so." Marcel listened and felt more assured that the town's detectives would be able to find his precious daughter. He disappeared into the kitchen for a moment and returned to the foyer carrying Clover's old laptop under one arm.

"We'll also need to search her desktop PC for possible leads," Detective Murphy added. With each passing moment the Baggards' lives were becoming more and more of a nightmare.

As Marcel held Hagatha, he gazed into her eyes and was startled by her vacant stare. Suddenly, her face was like a mask, strangely devoid of animation. "Shock," Marcel thought. "What can I do?" He handed the laptop to Detective Murphy. He stood as if he were in a bubble, watching the group of officers confer, unable to make out what they were saying, as if his brain had just stopped processing words and he could no longer understand what was going on around him.

Loralee's family was so disturbed by Clover's disappearance that their household was turned upside-down. The thought of Loralee going missing occurred to them, and just the idea of it was almost as disturbing as Clover actually disappearing.

"I don't understand," Loralee told her mother in tears, "I left her at the door and she didn't say she was going anywhere. But this time I didn't go inside. We were talking and I went only as far as the front door, Mom. She was fishing for her keys in her bag when I turned around to go down the stairway. I heard her phone make the sound it does when she gets a text."

Evelyn asked, "Why wouldn't she have gone in?"

"I don't know! All she said was that she'd see me later, and then her phone signaled that she'd received a text. She was so excited about her birthday. She wouldn't have gone anywhere!" Loralee stated loudly in frustration.

"I should've gone inside—we could've done our homework together!"

"Have a cup of chamomile tea and rest," Evelyn suggested. "Your father and I are going to take turns searching."

"No thanks, Mom, I don't want tea. I want my friend back! I want to go with you and Dad," Loralee begged her parents. "Please!"

"No honey, I want you to stay put. Please try not to worry. You should stay home in case Clover calls or comes by. Aunty Bev is on her way here to be with you."

"Does she have to? She never stops talking."

"Keep the doors locked. She has her own key. Please, don't be upset . . . but the police have found Clover's phone in the bushes by the front door. They can retrieve all her calls and texts," Evelyn said to console her daughter. "They'll find her."

Although they tried, Evelyn and Robert, Loralee's dad, couldn't reassure her enough. Loralee was frightened and in shock. Her dad said, "Don't worry, she'll show up. She's a clever young lady." No words could comfort her. Loralee was miserable and sad, trying to hold back the torrent of tears that wanted to flow down her face.

At the Baggards' house, Hagatha felt helpless, especially when the police told her, "Stay home and wait inside Mrs. Baggard, in case Clover calls home."

"I want to help," Hagatha pleaded desperately. "We can't just sit here doing nothing. Our baby is out there!"

"Yes, Ma'am."

Marcel was anxious and flatly stated, "I want to go looking for my daughter with the others. I can't just helplessly sit here!"

Lieutenant Freeman strongly suggested, "Mr. Baggard, I think it's best if you remain with your wife unless there's another relative who could stay with her." Marcel knew Hagatha was too panicky to be left alone so he agreed reluctantly. "Okay Lieutenant Freeman, I'll stay home and keep my wife company while we wait."

"We're checking your daughter's phone records, every call, one by one. It takes time." "And we'll get a tech on the computer," one of the officers said. "It doesn't look like anything is obviously out of place in the house, Mrs. Baggard."

"Yes, we know," Hagatha replied.

Hagatha repeatedly apologized to her husband for not calling sooner. She lamented, "I'm so sorry Marcel for not letting you know sooner that Clover was missing. I just kept thinking she would walk through the door and the nightmare would be over. It was wrong of me to wait."

Marcel held Hagatha's hand, gently squeezing it while he repeated how sorry he was for raising his voice. "Forgive me my love . . . please? I love you, dear, and nothing in this world matters more to me than you and Clover." Both were strangers to the uncertainty of such a frightening situation.

Marcel looked directly into Hagatha's sad, lost eyes as he asked her, "How can this be?" Neither of them moved, but instead stood still in an embrace, realizing again that they were living in a nightmare. Both of them wanted the living hell to end NOW! The sound of the phone ringing was like a blast penetrating the silence of the moment. Hagatha jumped!

It was Marcel's friend from work, calling to volunteer his time to look for Clover or to stay with

Hagatha if Marcel wanted to join any of the search parties himself. Marcel thanked him for his thoughtful gesture before hanging up, telling him that he would stay with Hagatha for now, but if his friend wanted to join the volunteers to search areas outside of town he would certainly be welcome.

One of Clover's books was on the coffee table and caught Marcel's eye. He picked it up, running his fingers over the cover, thinking that perhaps the book held some clue to her disappearance. "My emotions are so confused," Marcel admitted to Hagatha. "One minute I believe she will be coming home and the next I lose all hope. I don't know what to do. I feel so totally helpless."

Hagatha slowly shook her head from side to side without making a sound. He felt the same way she did: lost, shocked, confused, and emotionally exhausted.

Evelyn and Robert were too upset to stay home any longer and wait for Aunt Bev to arrive. They took Loralee with them until Aunt Bev was in the house and called. Robert left a note on the kitchen table for her to read once she entered the house in case she forgot what they told her, as she often did.

They were all compelled by their own discomfort to sit with the Baggards for a while before Evelyn joined her husband, who was leaving to go with a small group of neighbors walking alongside the edge of the woods that bordered two-lane highways. Robert had taken his heavy work gloves to fish through twigs and leaves for clues in his search for Clover.

Evelyn wasn't able to reassure her daughter enough and she thought that being closer to Hagatha might help her feel closer to Clover.

Marcel made Loralee a cup of hot chocolate with marshmallows, which was her favorite drink when she came over to do homework with Clover. He made steaming hot coffee for everyone else. The aroma of the coffee was calming as the vintage percolator bubbled and finished brewing the coffee. He carefully poured the imported coffee into mugs, thinking about the way Clover would beg for a small amount whenever she smelled the coffee percolating. Hagatha would always say, "You can wait to have that habit until after you graduate." And Clover would smile in response, saying, "That'll be sooner than later, Mom."

Little did Hagatha know that Clover and Loralee were already in the habit of sitting in the Starbucks next to the bakery, taking turns sipping an extra-large decaf and sharing a blueberry muffin or a slice of pumpkin cake. Clover considered Starbucks an innocuous habit compared to smoking, which they'd tried only once. Clover and Loralee choked and coughed so much after they inhaled that it discouraged both of them from ever trying again.

Loralee kept blaming herself for Clover's disappearance, thinking that she should have stayed with Clover and gone inside the house instead of dropping her off at the front door and going home.

"She's my best friend," Loralee managed to say in between sobs. "I watched her feeling through the stuff inside her bag for the keychain to unlock the door. I was sure she was planning on going inside. She would've called or texted me if she were in trouble, wouldn't she? I called every friend I could think of and no one has seen her! I am so sorry!"

Evelyn still wasn't having much success calming Loralee. She was as inconsolable as the Baggards.

Marcel thought that Loralee looked faint, so he brought a cold cloth for Evelyn to press against her daughter's forehead, and a paper bag in case Loralee hyperventilated. He recalled the time Loralee had a panic attack when she and her mother were visiting, and Evelyn used a paper bag to get her breathing under control. The same reaction occurred when she and Clover went to an amusement park and Marcel met them at the foot of the roller coaster once their ride had finished. He remembered using Clover's popcorn bag to regulate Loralee's breathing as she gasped for air. The doctors said it was mild asthma, but most of it was anxiety and too much stimulation. Hagatha watched silently, and though feeling rather helpless herself, she knew she had to make an effort to console her daughter's best friend.

Loralee apologized again and again for Clover's disappearance. Hagatha hugged her and explained to Loralee that it wasn't her fault; it was unreasonable to put the responsibility for whatever had happened to Clover on herself. "It could've happened to anyone. She'll be home soon," Hagatha said. "Maybe the excitement of her birthday has scrambled her thinking so that she's forgotten to call and tell us where she is. I'm sure there's an explanation, my dear child," Hagatha told her with deepest sincerity. "Please, don't take Clover's disappearance as your fault in any way." Hagatha paused for a moment, not wanting to upset Loralee further, but she was desperately trying to find answers and asked, "Did either of you meet someone new online?"

"No, we didn't, and I'm pretty sure that Clover would've told me if she did," Loralee stated with no doubt in her mind. "She's like my sister. We tell each other everything, Mrs. B."

Hagatha thought out loud, saying, "Both of you walk home together every day, the same time and going along the same route. Did you notice anything out of the ordinary?"

"No, I don't think so. I would've told you right away if I saw anything that was strange. Sometimes we take different routes, but not that often. And we both let each other know where we're going."

"With all the excitement, you might have forgotten to pay attention," Hagatha suggested.

"Mrs. B., we're always aware of our surroundings. It's been drilled into our heads since grammar school by you and my mom."

Hagatha gave a knowing smile and Evelyn rested her hand on Loralee's shoulder to comfort her. "Clover must have gone out after she came home, that's the only thing I can think of. And the one reason she might have left would be to look at dogs.

That's what I think. She really wanted a pup, Mrs. B.," Loralee stated with no doubt in her mind.

"Yes, I know," Hagatha said. "I knew we should've gotten her a dog a long time ago. Maybe she'd be here now if we had given her a dog earlier. We were planning on surprising her with a dog for Christmas this year."

"Clover is going to be thrilled—I can't wait to see her face! A dog! Don't worry, I won't tell her," Loralee innocently said. For a moment, she'd pushed the painful reality of her friend's situation from her mind. Frightened by the unknown, Loralee preferred believing that Clover wasn't missing. Hagatha and Evelyn forced smiles on their faces for Loralee's sake.

Evelyn turned to Hagatha and said, "Have you picked out a dog already?"

"No, we were waiting until Christmas."

A tear formed at the corner of Hagatha's eye and rolled down her cheek. She hurried upstairs to hide her tear-filled eyes. She went up to Clover's room looking for her daughter's favorite stuffed animal, but as she entered the room she felt a sharp pain in her back and chest and she began to breathe in shallow, quick breaths. She sat on the bed for a brief moment.

After regaining her composure, she returned downstairs and handed the old stuffed black dog with several discolored white spots to Loralee, who hugged the animal to her chest. "Keep Sammy for Clover until she comes home," Hagatha said. "She'd want you to take care of him for her."

Loralee hugged Hagatha just like Clover would have done if she received a surprise. Hagatha returned the embrace, hugging Loralee even tighter.

"Thanks, Mrs. B. I will cherish it."

Aunt Bev had called Evelyn. Mother and daughter stood by the door to leave. Loralee smiled, her face wet with tears as she hugged Hagatha one more time before leaving to go home. Robert had been talking to Marcel in the kitchen. Evelyn wasn't aware that Robert hadn't left to search for Clover yet. He could see that Marcel needed a friend. On the Baggards' porch on their way down the front stairs, Loralee told her parents about how much Clover was looking forward to getting her own dog. "Dad," Loralee said, "she was certain that this year wouldn't be the year, but she was wrong. Mrs. B. said they were buying her a dog after all, and to think how bummed out she was before, thinking that it wasn't going to ever happen. But she'd never run away because of that. When she gets home she'll be *so* happy. Boy—will she be surprised!"

Robert said, "Marcel and I have been discussing Clover. She would never leave her mom and dad intentionally."

"No she wouldn't, Dad, just like I would never leave you and Mom."

Hagatha and Marcel watched them as they walked down the stairway to the dimly lit street.

"I'll join you later on, Robert!" Marcel shouted.

"No! Stay with your wife. There are plenty of

people out there already."

Loralee turned around to speak to Mr. Baggard. The uncertainty in her voice was evident as she called to him, "Clover is coming home. Isn't she, Mr. B.?"

Marcel forced a smile. "Of course she is," he replied, "of course she is. She's out late, that's all." Hagatha wanted to agree, but she couldn't get the words out to respond. She nodded yes, wanting to placate her, but then she turned her face away so that Loralee wouldn't see the distress she was feeling. Suddenly, her home was bereft of children. To Hagatha, the rooms in her house were as empty as a nest from which the young had flown, hollow spaces without life or laughter. The reason for her being was no longer there, and she was in misery.

Time passed by and all they could do was wait.

Hagatha paced up and down the stairs, inside the house and outside.

Marcel wasn't able to keep up with her. He went down to the street, calling out his daughter's name but staying in view of his home. Hagatha and Marcel were restless. Clover's friends came by to give them support. So many people came that faces seemed to blend into one another. Each one told Hagatha where Clover was and what she was doing the last time they saw her. It was heartbreaking.

Seeing the length of the line at their door, Marcel returned to his wife and could tell by Hagatha's expression that she'd had enough of speaking with everyone. Marcel knew that he had to protect his wife's feelings. He bundled up to go down to the sidewalk to intercept people before they could get close to the front porch, explaining that she couldn't speak to anyone at this time. He noticed that the blank expression had returned to her face and he considered that the stare might be an indication that she was overwhelmed and shock was setting in to stay.

Their visitors were still attempting to converse with a woman they all knew well, but who had strangely turned into a stone figure. Hagatha, who was standing at the front screen door, finally opened it and went outside to the porch. Although it was freezing cold outside and she wasn't wearing a coat, she refused to go back inside the house. Marcel contended with the constantly ringing phone and the neighbors who were climbing up the front steps to the door by taping a "Do Not Disturb" sign at the bottom, where a stone wall bordered the sidewalk.

It was late and he was grateful there were fewer calls and less people stopping by. He recognized that Hagatha wasn't in any condition to be alone and that he had to remain by her side. He hung her warm coat on her shoulders like a shawl, knowing that she was oblivious to the weather. Marcel coaxed her, saying, "Hagatha, put your arms through the sleeves. Let me put your coat on you properly." She shook her head no.

Hagatha just stood outside, believing that Clover was alone somewhere out there in the dark, exposed to the cold, and she didn't want to be warm while her daughter might be freezing. The mere thought of it was upsetting beyond words.

"Dear, Clover dressed warmly enough today," Marcel assured his wife. "You're always reminding her to take a sweater and you know she wears thermal shirts, layers of jerseys, and leggings with those warm Ugg boots."

Hagatha barely nodded her head. As long as Clover was missing, she would stubbornly remain outside, going in the house only to use the bathroom and then coming back out again into the bitterly cold weather. She refused to be warm, preferring to suffer because it eased her deep emotional pain.

Marcel brought out her down coat, pillows and blankets, plus tea and soup to keep her warm. She took nothing for herself except for one of Clover's pillows and a worn blanket that was fifteen years old—Clover's baby blanket. This blanket was soothing to Hagatha in the same way a bottle of warm milk might comfort a baby. Marcel watched her every move as she twisted and turned, holding the baby blanket close to her mumbling, "It's my baby's birthday."

"Yes it is, Hagatha," Marcel replied. He folded one of his coats and tucked it under the cushion for her to sit on for insulation. He owned several cold weather jackets, shearling and down jackets that stood up to frigid temperatures when camping. Whenever the Baggards brought Loralee camping in Maine with them, she wore Marcel's shearling jacket that she said kept her so warm it was as if the animal skin was part of her.

Hagatha wrapped Clover's blanket high up around her shoulders and neck. She shut her eyes but her restlessness didn't allow her to sleep. Her heart was beating unusually fast, and it reverberated in her chest the way it did when she drank too many cups of coffee or had an occasional espresso. Instead of falling asleep, she sat there and recalled the night Clover was born, how worried Marcel was when her water broke and how joyful he was once Clover was free from the womb.

"It's a baby girl!" the doctor called out. She remembered her baby swaddled in the handmade blanket Marcel brought to the hospital with him. She pictured Clover's angelic face framed by the blanket, a pastel knitted masterpiece of green, yellow, and pink stars on a white background. It was a one-of-a-kind blanket the owner of the baby specialty shop sold to Hagatha, a place that was off to the side of a back road now long forgotten by the contemporary world. Hagatha thought back, about the store and its owner.

The store had been in business for over fifty years. She remembered the owner, Esther, who told her that she would be retiring in another year. Hagatha was amazed by the woman's attractiveness and spunkiness. It was a retirement that was well deserved. She looked as if she could be eighty years old, and as they spoke she learned that the old woman was actually ninety-six. "You look amazing!" Hagatha exclaimed. She wondered if she had a business, would she have the stamina to work that long. Esther said that after her children left for college, she opened the store. It had been her lifelong dream, just as opening the barn store was Hagatha's dream too.

Hagatha could sense the abundant energy emanating from her, and was happy and grateful to be in her company. She thought that the woman looked so youthful because her happiness shone through. Hagatha and Esther spoke about the history of the store for a while, and the woman gave her a few pieces of baby furniture—a crib and a rocking chair that had been used for display for many years. Esther told Hagatha about her grandchildren and great-grandchildren, none of whom had the slightest interest in running a small business like her own.

The store was a labor of love, she explained to Hagatha, "A piece of you goes out to every one of your customers, whether they buy or just look. It's an exchange of energy." Their conversation was like a talk between two long-lost friends.

Hagatha stayed for a few hours before she looked at the time, saying, "Oh my, I have to go now." She thanked the woman and gave her a warm hug, adding that she intended to refinish and paint the old, but not forgotten, antique pieces.

"Someday I'll have a dream like yours to see through to its fulfillment. I'm leaving here with a piece of you, I suppose. I'll mail you a photo of the finished pieces. I won't forget you." Hagatha's sentiment touched the old woman, "I'm happy to give you and your baby something to remember."

Hagatha considered herself fortunate to be able to buy the blanket there, and had also selected a knitted outfit for her yet-to-be-born baby to wear home from the hospital. She recalled how soft it felt. She also recalled Esther's heartfelt last words to her: "You and your baby will always be happy together and your relationship will be close." Hagatha waved, and always remembered Esther's blessing.

All these years later she could still smell Clover's unique ivory-rose scent as she held the worn blanket close, with all of its fond memories of her daughter. She pictured her three-year-old daughter clutching the blanket, trailing it behind her, dragging and tugging it everywhere she went. Clover would ask for her "Esther" and Hagatha knew immediately that she wanted her favorite blanket. Even as worn and pilled as the blanket became over the years, Clover kept it as a reminder of her happy childhood and her mother's care. It was Clover's prized "Esther" and Hagatha tried to keep it in as good condition as she could, laundering it ever so carefully with especially mild soap.

Hagatha recalled the evening when Clover told her how she was planning to save the blanket for her first child. She wanted to redesign the original knitting with borders made from old clothes she kept from her childhood, stitching different patterns to the worn edges. Clover had started the project a year ago, but finished only one side.

"You still have plenty of years to finish it," Hagatha would tell her. Clover was even going to order a nametag to sew onto the blanket that said "Esther." Hagatha used to tell Clover the story about the old woman who had given her the furniture, and how important the pieces were to her. Once Hagatha refinished the pieces, she sent Esther a photograph of the restored furniture along with a picture of baby Clover, and a note that said, "You will always be in my thoughts and your beautiful furniture will still be here for my grandchildren yet to be born." The old woman sent a card back expressing her thanks. Clover kept the card with all of her own possessions.

CHAPTER 4

MIDNIGHT COME AND GONE

Hagatha pictured her mom and dad, the proud grandparents of their precious granddaughter. She dreaded the Happy Birthday telephone calls that she knew would be coming from her parents and Marcel's parents and family. The first time her father saw Clover, he cried. He took her in his arms and caressed her just as he had done to Hagatha when she was an infant. Hagatha's mom often recalled this scene with delight.

Hagatha hadn't called her parents about Clover's disappearance yet, not wanting to worry her family before there was more hopeful information. The police had informed them that they would send out an alert after 24 hours had passed and they were sure that Clover was indeed missing. She thought about her parents coming for Christmas to celebrate the holiday, Clover's birthday, and the opening of the barn store. Hagatha glanced at her watch. It was after midnight and Clover had just turned sixteen.

Telling her parents that Clover was missing terrified her and Marcel.

Hagatha spoke to the blanket, asking for Clover to come home. "Please," she begged. "Please! My baby, it's your birthday!" It was already December fifteenth. She rocked back and forth singing the lullaby she used to sing to Clover.

Marcel, who was sitting next to her, observed her highly emotional state and was concerned for his wife. She sang the lullaby softly as her husband listened. He pictured Clover as an infant wrapped in Hagatha's arms. Then he quickly returned to reality, as if it had slapped him across the face. A small Sweet Sixteen Birthday Party—today! Clover had invited her closest friends over to the house to celebrate in advance of the party that would take place later on at Christmastime. Marcel thought about his beautiful daughter, and how she had gone missing on her own special day. He knew he had to maintain a brave exterior for Hagatha despite his confusion, regret, and fatigue. "She would never miss her own party intentionally," he thought to himself.

"She'll be home soon, dear," he said, "you must believe this." For a brief moment he thought it was possible that Clover had mentioned where she was going and their memories had failed them. Marcel wondered if Clover had slipped out to have a celebratory drink in another town with someone of drinking age. She had talked about that at the dinner table several times saying, archly, "I will act the part of a sophisticated lady and order a martini!"

"Do you think she wanted to be with a new friend today?" Hagatha asked.

"Who would that be?" Marcel questioned. Then he realized how ridiculous his thinking had become; he just wished it wasn't true that Clover had vanished. He looked up at the clearing night sky and the multitude of stars. Hagatha always made sure she was aware of all the places Clover went, and Marcel knew this. Maybe she had gone to a store to buy her mother an early present for Christmas with the extra cash she saved, and had been shopping at the mall until it closed. But it was long after the 10 p.m. closing time. Where could she be? Although Clover wasn't the type of person who would go out without telling someone, he was trying as best he could to find plausible reasons for her to be missing. He searched for reasons that would account for her lateness coming home, not her disappearance.

Marcel climbed the stairs to Clover's bedroom, to where she had a hiding place for her money. Hagatha wasn't aware of her daughter's secret cash and he hadn't informed the police of it either. The money was hidden deep in her closet, inside a cookie tin on the highest shelf. Clover told her dad that she'd been saving money to buy a gift for her mom. Marcel opened the tin and saw that her money was still there, every last cent of it rolled in a hair ribbon she had fashioned from velvet and lace. He felt helpless, like he was adrift at sea. Wavering between hope and despair, he went back downstairs, where he took his place next to Hagatha, holding her hand as much for his own consolation as hers.

Marcel remembered that Clover and her friends had been planning for weeks to get together at their house the day of her birthday—a small gathering with a cake. "Yes . . . the cake," he thought. They were supposed to pick it up; it was either yesterday or today, in the morning. He couldn't recall the exact time they would be celebrating, maybe four or five. Marcel looked up the email about it on his phone so that he could write them a reply to put a hold on the cake until they heard from him further. He would call later on, during store hours. Marcel's heart skipped a beat. "She would never miss her own party intentionally," he thought. "She'd never miss the chocolate cake!"

Silently, he wished for Clover to call. "Please, baby girl! Call me!" Usually, Marcel was at a loss for words when he tried to pray, but tonight was different and the words flowed, pleading over and over to Clover's angels for her to come home. "We are so worried," he whispered out loud.

Hagatha peered over the blanket to glance at her husband. He said, "She may be at some new friend's house . . . " The silence between himself and Hagatha was intolerable, and hung heavily between them like wet sheets on a clothesline. Neither of them mentioned the fact that Clover's phone had been found in the bushes. Marcel finally felt compelled to speak. "If she went to a store, then went to a friend's house and fell asleep there," he said, "she wouldn't be home until the morning. Don't you think so, dear?"

Hagatha was mired in her own inner world and didn't respond beyond a nod of her head.

Marcel stood and went inside the house to find his other warm coat. The temperature was dropping and it was brutally cold. His fears turned his blood colder. He felt chilled, and visibly shook. He looked one more time at the caller ID on the phone. He knew it was going to be a long night until the sun came up. The house was dark except for one lamp in the living room, a lamp with beaded tassels on the lampshade. The reflection of the lampshade played on the wall and looked like falling tears to Marcel as he walked slowly by. Each second that passed was like a bomb ticking; he almost lost his faith, doubting his belief that Clover would come home.

The police returned at about three in the morning to say that the neighborhood search party had gone home to rest and would start again early in the day.

The Baggards sat up straight, stunned, wearing lost expressions as if they were standing before a firing squad.

Lieutenant Freeman explained, "Clover's recent phone calls didn't yield any clues to her whereabouts. Nor had she visited any hospital emergency rooms. We're continuing to look into the number for the prepaid phone that called in when she was with her friend at the door." They had scoured the entire town, thirty square miles that included several parks and an area of thick woods.

Emerson was predominantly residential, with a commercial main street and a few small pockets of industry—a typical Massachusetts town.

Hagatha was becoming hysterical, repeating, "How can this be?" over and over again. "When Loralee said Clover received a text when she was at the door with her, you don't know who that was?"

"No, Ma'am, not yet," an officer said.

Lieutenant Freeman added, "We haven't been able to determine who sent it. The caller used a prepaid phone from an unknown number. We're checking out the number through the phone service. Although prepaid phones aren't impossible to trace, they are harder and more time-consuming to track."

"We have to keep looking," Hagatha insisted, "please don't give up! She may be sick, lying on the ground somewhere unable to move! My baby could be in trouble!" She was screaming, "Someone must know . . . please! Why aren't you able to find the number of the text?" Hagatha was losing it. She pulled the corner of Clover's baby blanket so forcefully that all the pillows fell to the porch floor. "Let me help you," the lieutenant said, leaning over.

"No, no, Lieutenant," Marcel replied. "I'll take care of it . . . "

Marcel was angry with the police and agreed with his wife, saying, "You can't stop looking—please! These hours are crucial! I'll go." He demanded that he be allowed to go with them to look. "Could somebody stay with my wife? I can't call anyone to come at this hour." "There are officers still out there, Mr. Baggard, calm down," the lieutenant told them. "We are continuing to look. We won't give up; we want to find your daughter too. I didn't mean for it to sound like we stopped, sir. I apologize to you both. The folks from town went home, not the police officers. They're on this 24/7."

Marcel sighed in relief, as did Hagatha. "We're sorry, Mr. Baggard. We're trying not to alarm or frighten you." Marcel regretted his outburst and apologized for himself and Hagatha. He said nothing more. He thought that just the police searching wasn't enough, that more people needed to be out looking for her. He had to contact an agency with private detectives first thing in the morning; they would be necessary to find Clover if she wasn't home by 9 a.m.

Lieutenant Freeman had been speaking on his phone to the carrier for the prepaid phone and added, "The text Clover received at the time Loralee left her at the door said, 'Hi Clove, Happy B-day.'" The lieutenant said that he wished he had more information for them, but reassured Hagatha and Marcel, "The techs are working on it. They retrieved the message but haven't identified the sender yet. Don't you worry, as soon as we know we'll tell you right away."

"The state police have been notified," another officer told them. "We have only four manned patrol cars in Emerson, but we'll have ten more in about thirty minutes. They'll work with us from here on in to locate your daughter—around the clock."

Marcel asked, "Have other law enforcement agencies been contacted?"

"Yes, some twenty surrounding towns. Believe me Mr. Baggard, we are all devoting ourselves to your daughter's case, and will continue until she's found. Please trust us and try to get some rest. The majority of us have children and understand how upsetting this must be for you."

As Hagatha extended her cold, trembling hand to the officer, he cupped both hands firmly over hers to console her, sensing the depth of her pain as she broke down and cried. He stepped back as Marcel came to her aid and guided her to the white wicker armchair, gently helping her to be seated. The officer had tears in his eyes as well, thinking not only of Clover's disappearance but the very real possibility of losing his own children.

"Clover's friends provided us with ample leads and we're following all of them," Lieutenant Freeman assured Marcel and Hagatha. "We'll do whatever it takes. We'll be using all our resources to find your daughter. Volunteers from the fire department will be working with us in our search efforts." Marcel thanked the lieutenant.

Despite his frustration, Marcel realized the officer was right. They were able to cover far more ground than he could. He appreciated having help from the internet in this respect, posting Clover's photograph on social sites for people to see and perhaps reach out and assist them in their search.

"It's her birthday," Hagatha told the officer. "It's

today." Marcel realized that he and Hagatha needed to have greater faith in the ability of the police to find their daughter. Hagatha held out her hand to Marcel and, clutching it, Marcel asked her if she heard and understood what the officer told her.

"I did," she said, "I know there *is* hope that Clover will come home. She has her belief in angels and we believe in her."

Hagatha sat with her coat on and the baby blanket draped around her shoulders. She wasn't dressed warmly enough for the night's low temperature. The police made an effort to persuade Hagatha to go inside, but she refused. Marcel couldn't convince Hagatha to stop her vigil either. He carried down several more of Clover's quilts and blankets from her room to cover his wife, but her shivering was so extreme that she began shaking uncontrollably and her ruddy cheeks turned pale. Her teeth began chattering and her tired eyes opened and closed.

All Marcel could do was watch and pray. Hagatha was tightly bundled in all of Clover's covers and felt close to her daughter, smelling the fragrance, trying to catch her daughter's scent in the brisk, cold air. When she rested her head on Clover's pillow, she breathed in her daughter's distinctive sweet fragrance, a combination of Clover's smell laced with Betsey Johnson and Juicy perfume. Clover loved the charms that hung from the Juicy Couture bottles. Hagatha believed she was in her daughter's presence, imagining that she was there. She spoke to her daughter tenderly as tears rolled down her cheeks.

She tucked one of Clover's baby toys close to her heart—it was a small rag doll her grandmother Maura had given her.

Marcel coaxed Hagatha into sitting on Clover's favorite swing chair for fifteen minutes before she went back to the wicker chair. "It'll help you relax," he whispered. "Please?" Hagatha moved to the swing willingly. The double cushions that Marcel's mother had made out of down feathers and polyester were so plush they kept Hagatha just as warm as Marcel's folded, down coat. He covered her with more stuffed animals and pillows from Clover's bed not only for warmth, but to have Clover's things closer to her. He even brought an electric heater outside to protect his wife against the freezing temperature. It enveloped her in a small pocket of warmth that drifted by her, carried by a slight breeze. But Hagatha was unaware.

To Marcel, she looked numb, as though she was still suffering from some sort of paralysis. He sat beside her huddled in silence, looking up at the stars and at her. Her stare was blank. Marcel placed his hand across Hagatha's chest and felt her heart beating slowly, as if she were calmer or resting. Marcel told Hagatha he would go search for Clover in spite of what the police said, but only if she agreed to go inside and lock the doors until his friend came in the morning. She refused to leave the porch and said, "I'm afraid. What if *you* don't come back? I don't want any friends here. I don't want anyone to come here."

"Hagatha, I'll be back. I could never leave you. I love you more than life itself," stated Marcel.

"I don't want to stay with your friend," she said. "With both of you not here I'll worry even more." Because of her fragility, Marcel decided to stay close to his wife. "Hagatha," he remarked, "I'm here with you. I won't go." She calmed down from the panic she initially felt. Marcel remarked, "We'll welcome Clover home together."

Morning was fast approaching. It was past six when the first light of dawn appeared. When she dozed off, Marcel left her side to call her family, whom he woke from a sound sleep, as well as his own parents in France, where it was approaching mid-day. He constantly paced to the front window with the cordless phone at his ear to check on Hagatha, not wanting to stand too close and have his conversation wake her up.

Her mother was alarmed not only because she was awakened by the phone, but more so because Clover had been missing for hours and on her sixteenth birthday. She was horrified. "Oh my God, my poor Haggy!" she whispered into the phone not wanting to wake her husband, who had been ill. "And my precious granddaughter . . . where is she?"

"I hope I didn't call too early for you. I know you're both early risers," Marcel said.

"We were up late last night, but you know you can call anytime." Hagatha's father awoke and his wife told him about what had happened. Both were anxious and wanted to come over right away to do whatever they could to help. Marcel's parents were shocked by his news, but once they collected themselves, they offered to leave immediately despite the distance and expense.

"We want to be there for the two of you," his mother said.

"Clover will be back soon, and she'll study in Paris one day," Marcel stated, trying to keep them calm. He explained to both sets of grandparents that Hagatha's condition was too sensitive for her to have any company and that she preferred being by herself; he would keep in touch with them daily until Clover came home. Hagatha's mother promised to call other members of the family to let them know about Clover.

Hagatha's father called back to argue that he would like to visit, regardless of Hagatha's state of mind, but Marcel dissuaded him from coming because of his father-in-law's weak heart and asked him to be patient. "Please, Dad," Marcel said, "we can't have you getting sick again. Those are your daughter's wishes."

"But we should be there!" he argued. In the background, Marcel could hear his mother-in-law's tormented sobbing. He knew Hagatha's father was sickly and was afraid his condition would only become worse with worry—seeing his daughter in her present state might weaken him further. He asked both sets of parents to call him on his cell phone rather than the house line because Hagatha became startled every time the phone rang.

Replacing the phone in its base, Marcel exhaled deeply, shaking his head from side to side, doubting that he could deal with the whole situation.

Suddenly, he was overcome by a wave of anger and frustration. He pressed his forehead closely against the wall, banging it again and again in a slow rhythm. He began to weep. His clenched fist pounded the door until his knuckles were red and almost bloodied. The throbbing pain of his hand brought his attention back to the present situation— his dear wife on the porch in the cold.

He thought of Clover and pulled himself together for her sake. Despite his anger, he picked up the phone and called a few other relatives to tell them about Clover. Marcel watched the sunlight reflecting off the walls in the hallway. The morning traffic cast shadows as the cars drove by on their way to work or school. It was striking to him that life continued to go on when to him all normality had stopped. The sun had not yet fully risen on the cold, early morning and Marcel thought how it would be approaching its brightest at around noontime.

A cruiser pulled up in front of the house at 8 a.m. and the chief of police, Chief Henley, got out and waited on the steps for Marcel to come outside. He glanced at Hagatha wrapped up in a bundle of covers, hoping that the expression on her face meant that she was asleep. Chief Henley greeted Marcel, touching his arm as a sign of camaraderie, and explained in a low whisper that there had been many policemen from the town working throughout the night and morning, and there would be more officers from surrounding towns and cities joining all through the day. "No news yet," he cautiously stated.

Hagatha sat up without any expression on her face. The chief nodded and asked her how she was feeling. She barely understood that Chief Henley was addressing her and struggled to find words to respond to him.

When Marcel saw that his wife couldn't answer, he apologized to the chief, "I'm sorry, all of this has taken us totally by surprise, and unfortunately Hagatha is experiencing an extreme emotional response." Hagatha corrected her posture and, still holding onto the blankets wrapped around her, tried to listen more closely. She was able to hear some of their conversation; her eyes were glazed over from lack of sleep and emotional shock. The words between the Chief of Police and Marcel bounced off her like vibrations against a wall. Chief Henley turned and explained to her, "The members of the neighborhood search parties who have children went home to resume their schedules. They needed to go back to work and send their children off to school, albeit reluctantly because of Clover's disappearance. Other members of the search party, particularly those who don't have children, stayed out longer and went to work without sleeping at all last night. You have very loyal and faithful neighbors and friends. They promised to resume searching after work again today if Clover hasn't been found yet."

"Thanks so much," Marcel said with genuine gratitude.

Marcel thought about how he hadn't seen Clover for twenty-four hours, since she left for school the day before. "Where is our daughter?" he asked the chief, "How much longer before she returns?"

"Sir," Chief Henley replied, "I really can't say. We're doing our best to locate her."

As Marcel and Chief Henley stood at the front door, the chief noticed his injured fist. It was extremely swollen. "Do you want to see a doctor, Sir?"

"No, no. I'm just fine, thanks."

"Believe me, Mr. Baggard," the chief continued, "The people of this town are angry, and eager to help in any way they can. They're committed. They'll spend every spare minute they have searching for your daughter. I understand that one of your neighbors has postponed their Christmas vacation plans in Europe, saying that finding your daughter is more important than their trip. One of our officers can sit with your wife if you have any other matters to tend to inside, like taking care of that hand."

"No, thanks, I appreciate it, though. My wife gets nervous when I'm not around."

"Would you mind telling me how that happened?" the officer asked. "I punched the wall," Marcel replied matter-of-factly.

"Sorry Sir, I had to ask."

"I understand," he replied. Marcel was consumed

by his desire to search along with the police. He kept asking but he finally realized what could happen: Hagatha could leave and wander aimlessly in an effort to find Clover. He couldn't bear losing them both.

"We've done all we can do for one night in the neighborhoods," the officer told him. "After the stores open it'll be easier to comb the towns." It was about nine in the morning. "The officers can bring you coffee, if you like. Dunkin' or Starbucks?"

"I appreciate your offer, but no, if anything, I should make some coffee for you. I travel all around the world and bring back quite an assortment," Marcel stated, wanting to show his thanks in some way but being unable to find the energy to even make a pot of coffee in his present condition—it was clearly out of the question. He had made coffee all during the night and was still exhausted.

"No thanks, Mr. Baggard. Just try to stay calm." Chief Henley excused himself and headed out to his car. He drove away, leaving two patrolmen in a car parked on the street in front of the house to watch and wait in case Clover came home. He then circled the block several times to make certain the officers were alert after being awake all night. Several empty coffee cups were scattered on the dashboard of the cruiser, with more littering the floor of the back seat.

There were no sounds as the Baggards sat together in the chilly morning watching pairs of birds flying from tree to tree and squirrels scampering along the ground looking for food.

Neighbors waved to them as they passed in their cars on their way to work. Both Hagatha and Marcel experienced feelings of emptiness. An abrupt end had come to their once-happy life.

The mist in the air had already evaporated and the light of the sun emerged from behind the clouds. It was wrenching for Marcel to watch Hagatha tossing and turning. She squinted, her eyes bothered by the rays of light filtering through. She was disturbed, and so agitated that her arms and legs thrashed underneath the weight of the heavy covers. "She must be half-asleep and having nightmares," Marcel thought. Then he checked his muted phone to see if the bakery had left him a message in response to his about cancelling Clover's cake. He knew that they started baking earlier than 5 a.m. on most days but probably wouldn't get their messages until they were ready to open.

Marcel stared at the blankets and toys while his mind wandered, traveling back to when Clover was an infant and the nurse at the hospital handed him his baby girl. He remembered holding her warm, swaddled body in his arms, her face so perfectly round and smooth with pink lips and rosy cheeks. He kissed her cheeks and forehead, speaking baby talk to her. "Oh, how pretty she was," he thought. His infant's eyes were bright and wide open, seemingly staring at her daddy. He could feel her wriggling even now—she was active from the start, and so strong that she nearly rolled off the table immediately after she was born as the nurses were cleaning her.

"This is our baby," he told Hagatha. "Look at what we've created—a beautiful baby girl!"

He remembered leaning over Hagatha and giving her a kiss out of love and admiration. Marcel marveled at her calm nature during Clover's birth and her composure in all crises, whether at school or home. When one of the nurses put Clover into her crib, Marcel freed her from the blanket and bent down to kiss each of her fingers. Then, he recalled, Clover curled her chubby fingers into a fist. "Oh, you're mad at your daddy so soon!" he told her with laughter and joy.

Then, as abruptly as they began, Marcel's musings ended, and he came back to the present. Here he was, sitting next to Hagatha on the swing in the cold, wanting to share his memories of Clover with her but hesitant out of fear of causing her greater emotional turmoil. Their daughter was older now—sixteen years old—and prone to do what teens do without their parents' permission. Not Clover, though; it was out of character for Clover to act out. Marcel clenched his fists. Not their Clover, never! "You've been out one entire night, just please, come home now," he thought to himself. "No punishment—just a hug!"

Just then Hagatha's eyes opened into a wide stare. She focused intently on Marcel, looking directly into his eyes, as if she knew his thoughts. He felt as though her gaze penetrated him to his soul. For a brief moment they were inextricably connected, and then she closed her eyes again, almost as if some greater force had shut them for her.

"She'll be home soon . . . " Marcel said, as he gazed at his wife's beautiful face. Marcel felt that since he came home from work the day before, each moment had lasted for an eternity. "This can't be real," he repeated inside his head. "This just can't be." He watched his wife as her movements became anguished and filled with pain.

"Hagatha, I love you so much," he whispered.

"I love you too," she mumbled with her eyes still tightly shut.

CHAPTER 5

SUNRISE AND BITTER COLD

Marcel snuggled closer to his wife so that both of them would feel warmer. The sadness they felt seemed to be infinite and totally overwhelming. Both had always felt as though they were joined together, yet now Marcel sensed something new, a distance between them, an unfamiliar feeling. Hagatha loosened her hand from underneath the blankets and clutched Marcel's hand like it was their last moment together. The heater Marcel had connected outside provided little warmth to counter the bitter cold morning. Both Hagatha and Marcel shivered as the blades of grass glistened between the snow patches, and in the sun's rays it was possible to see miniscule filaments of silver, slivers of light that gave the impression of tiny, elegant fairies dancing and twisting in the air.

Pressing his head against her chest, Marcel was alarmed as he listened to the rhythm of his wife's heart. It was again beating much faster than it normally should. Anguish and anxiety fueled the rapid pulsing. Marcel thought he should keep Hagatha busy to take her mind off Clover. He stood up and persuaded his wife to join him inside so that she could wash her face, brush her teeth, and have some hot decaf coffee—a cup without caffeine to keep her heart from racing faster than it was already beating.

"Come on, you don't have a choice," he stated, taking charge. He extended his hand out to her, pulling her up as she grasped Clover's blankets, holding them tight. They stood arm in arm and strode together into the warmth of the house.

Hagatha's movements were slow. She gave in to her husband's wishes only to make him happy and had little fight left in her. Marcel brought Hagatha, wearing her shawl of blankets, into the downstairs bathroom. Standing behind her in front of the mirror they gazed at their exhausted reflections. He filled the sink full of warm, soapy water and slowly washed his wife's face with a soft facecloth, stroking it like an artist creating a painting with his brush. He wiped the cloth over her neck, talking to her all the while to raise her spirits. He complimented her complexion, saying how lovely her skin was. "You are so beautiful," he told her. "I've thought so since the day we met."

"Thank you," she said in a low whisper.

"Sometimes I forget to tell you, but it's always in my mind."

"Yes," she answered, "I know." She was so weak

and lightheaded that her knees buckled and gave way. Marcel caught her in his arms and guided her down to a sitting position on the stool in the corner. As she leaned forward with her head lowered between her legs, the blankets slid to the floor, one layer at a time.

Marcel put a warm washcloth on her cool shoulders and massaged her calves, attempting to improve the flow of blood in her chilled body. Her torso collapsed, and she slumped over like a rag doll. Slowly he helped her to lift her head.

As he was kneeling in front of her, he said "Hagatha, What happened to your knee?" He noticed a small tear in the material of her pants with dried bloodstains. He rolled up her jeans and saw that her knee was swollen, bruised a deep blue, and had a red gash. "That's a nasty cut, shouldn't you go to the hospital?" he asked. "You need an x-ray," Marcel told her, "your knee is badly cut and bruised."

Hagatha snapped at him. "I will not leave this house!" she insisted. "Not until Clover comes home. I'm just fine. I don't feel any pain and I certainly don't care about a silly bruise." Hagatha vaguely remembered falling in the kitchen doorway. She hadn't felt any pain at the time, nor did she feel anything until Marcel mentioned it. Now she felt soreness as she touched her leg. Marcel helped Hagatha stand and supported her weight as they walked over to the living room couch.

"Lie down until I come back," he told her. "Don't

get up; just wait for me."

Marcel went upstairs first to get some warm flannel pajama bottoms of Clover's he knew Hagatha would agree to put on. Then he went into the kitchen, returned with a cloth for his wife, and applied alcohol and an ice bag to her knee, saying, "Honey, do you remember the first time Clover rode her two-wheel bicycle?" Hagatha nodded her head, sharing a warm and loving smile. "We watched her go down a slight incline on the sidewalk as we cheered her on. She was smiling, so confident. Then there was that split second when she turned her head back to see us, waving with one hand. She lost her balance and fell off onto the concrete. Both of us rushed to her . . ."

"I remember," Hagatha whispered. "Her right knee was scraped and swollen, just like yours is now," Marcel said. "We took her inside, propped her up on the couch, and put an ice bag on her knee, the same as we're doing to your knee. I panicked and said that we should go to the hospital, but you said, 'First, let's clean the wound and treat her knee with ice packs for a day and watch for any improvement, then decide whether to take her or not.' Do you remember?"

"Of course I do," Hagatha replied. "That's why I'm not going to the hospital," she said definitively. Hagatha knew the drill from school, where bruised and swollen knees were as frequent as recess. Marcel was glad Hagatha responded to the memory of Clover's injured knee with her usual good sense still intact. At the next moment, however, Hagatha's face froze into a vacant stare and she suddenly became quiet. Then her face twisted as if she were in pain.

"Are you okay, dear?" Marcel asked. He didn't receive a reply. He knew her knee hurt but didn't press her.

In her silence, Hagatha recalled the many times during Clover's childhood when she'd fallen and scraped her knees and elbows. Now she held the same bags of ice in place. She removed and reapplied them exactly as she had done for Clover all those times, although at this moment she wasn't conscious of what she was doing.

Marcel observed her closely. He was relieved that she was helping herself rather than showing little to no interest in her own welfare, but in her mind Hagatha was applying the ice to Clover's knee, not her own. "Hagatha, I'll stay right with you as long as it takes for the swelling to go down. Let's go in the sitting room. It's warmer and we can see out to the front and side doors."

While in the sitting room, out of nowhere, as if nothing were wrong, Hagatha suddenly snapped out of it and said, "Tell me, Marcel, how did I hurt my knee? I don't remember." Marcel noted that Hagatha was acting like herself again.

"I'm not sure myself," Marcel told her. "I wasn't home when you injured it. You really don't remember?"

"No, sorry. I don't," Hagatha said. She noticed the scrape on the knuckles of Marcel's fist. "Did you hurt your hand when I cut my knee?"

"No," he replied, "I didn't." Hagatha's question disturbed him. She was going in and out of reality.

"Marcel, I'd rather sit in Clover's room. I want to be near her, please?" Hagatha calmly asked. Marcel understood that Hagatha didn't want to stay in the sitting room any longer because that was where Clover was supposed to have had her birthday party with her friends. Hagatha wouldn't get to video the dress-up fashion show Clover had planned for her party, and she felt Clover's loss all too poignantly being in that room. "Let's go up to Clover's room, please?" she asked again.

They climbed the stairs and walked to Clover's door. Pushing the door open, Hagatha's eyes scanned the room and focused on one of Clover's belongings, then another.

"Remember the time we were at the beach and Clover slipped on those oversized, sharp rocks in the water and hit her head? I thought we'd lost her for a moment. The knot was the size of a golf ball," Hagatha remarked, "but she was fine then and she's fine now—just very late getting home. Isn't that right?" She turned to her husband for reassurance.

"Yes, she's just late getting home. And yes, I remember. We helped her back to the blanket. When I took the butter knife out of the picnic basket, Clover thought we were going to cut off the bump. She sprang up to her feet, holding her head. I remember her screaming. We reassured her that I was only going to press the bump and it wouldn't hurt that much, that the most she might feel would be a little discomfort. We laughed and laughed." Marcel smiled at the memory as he spoke.

"Yes, I certainly do remember that day," Hagatha said. "I felt badly for Clover, but it was amusing to watch her reaction. The bump became smaller and smaller, and . . . I . . . I . . . can't go on like this," Hagatha cried out, "please tell me they'll find her! Marcel, our daughter isn't home yet!" Both of them were overwhelmed by the pain in their hearts. Hagatha edged closer to her husband, and as he took her in his arms in a loving and sad embrace, their bodies touched. The first 24 hours had been sheer hell.

Clover's sixteenth birthday passed, and then a week of Hagatha being sick from staying out in the cold so long, and then more days went by. There was no sign of Clover. The police were in daily contact with the Baggards, but the reports were disheartening; they provided little hope. Search teams continued in their efforts. The FBI was brought in and the bureau directed resources to the search for Clover Baggard nationwide.

On alternate days, Marcel searched for Clover with various members of the family, who would wait in their cars in front of the house for him to come down. Hagatha didn't allow anyone near her except for her close neighbors Evelyn and Loralee, especially because Loralee was like a second daughter to her.

No progress had been made. There weren't any

leads. There seemed to be little reason for Hagatha to climb out of her deep depression. Evelyn and Loralee would sit with her day after day while Marcel went out looking for Clover. He was out for twenty hours a day sometimes, and his face looked haggard and old. Loralee convinced Hagatha to come inside the house from the freezing cold; her convalescence had been slow, yet still she went outside to look, half expecting to see Clover walking up toward the house. She spent a great deal of time curled up on the sofa in the living room, barely speaking. She only gave yes or no answers to the questions she was asked and replied to Loralee only.

Loralee discovered a way to persuade Hagatha to cooperate with her, and that was to say, "Clover would've wanted you to do this or that." Several family albums were piled on the end table, and Hagatha spent hours slowly turning the pages of photographs while Loralee told her stories about certain places and people in the snapshots. From time to time, she managed a slight smile and would extend her hand for Loralee to hold.

The couch in the living room was placed facing the front entrance so that Hagatha would have a direct line of sight when Clover came through the door. She stared out the window like a dog waiting for its owner to come home. Loralee babbled on about Clover, saying Clover this and Clover that, and what their plans were for the future. Hagatha paid attention to what she said. Loralee stayed by her side, always trying to elicit happy memories, and encouraging her to be positive.

Marcel stayed at home after weeks of searching so that Evelyn and Loralee could spend more time at home together with Robert, who often searched for Clover along with him. When Marcel was finally able to coax Hagatha off the sofa, she went upstairs to Clover's room, lying down tightly tucked into her bed while Marcel rocked in Clover's chair beside his wife.

"I was thinking it might be nice for your mother to visit us," said Marcel hopefully.

"You already know how I feel about that Marcel," she said. "I don't want anyone besides Loralee and Evelyn to visit until Clover comes home!" Hagatha stated angrily to him, showing her stubborn streak and total refusal to allow her mother to visit. She was neglecting her hygiene and Marcel had no choice other than to treat her like a child and wash her himself. Anger would fill the house, with Hagatha yelling and screaming—and this was followed by silence for the next few days.

The pain, emptiness, and sadness seemed endless and trickled into every nook and cranny in the entire house. How long would this go on? Would they ever see their precious daughter again? Where did she go? Why didn't anyone see her? Why hadn't Clover been found yet?

Loralee remembered that she and Clover had visited new sites on the internet and she told Marcel who, in turn, told the police. The police were familiar with some of the teen sites he mentioned and informed Marcel that they didn't pose any danger that they were aware of, but they would check Clover's computers again to be sure they hadn't missed anything. What they found were pages of vintage buttons shown on old factory sites, but that was all. Their investigation didn't produce any promising leads.

Hagatha walked around the house in a daze, constantly talking to herself, speaking only about subjects in which she and Clover shared an interest. She talked into thin air—discussing art, decorating, design, making clothes, making and decorating cupcakes—conversing with Clover as if she were standing there next to her. Hagatha told Clover not to fret because she'd missed her birthday party; she would make another one for her outside in the clover field next to the barn even though it was December and the weather was cold. Listening to her, there were brief moments when Marcel imagined that Clover was actually there.

Marcel was deeply concerned. He had to hire someone to clean the kitchen and bathrooms, and to keep an eye on his wife so that she wouldn't be alone when he went back to work. He found a gem of a cleaning woman who was sympathetic toward Hagatha and wonderfully adept at caring for her. She became more than a cleaning woman. Originally from Brazil, Sophia spoke only broken English. She would lead Hagatha to the bathroom singing softly and beautifully, and though she didn't understand Sophia's language the melodies soothed her if only for a short time. Sophia bathed her and would brush her hair with one of Clover's many hairbrushes as if Hagatha were a child herself.

Every minute Marcel spent away from Hagatha he felt guilty and tortured. He had to go back to work not only to make money, but because he felt his sanity was at stake. Hagatha had pushed him away as if he were some stranger. She lived in a world inside her head, and the more Marcel did to care for her, the worse she became. He couldn't bear pushing her to perform the basic tasks of living. Marcel felt as though he was stuck.

Marcel searched sites meant for teenagers on the computer. He was stunned by the access they had to drugs, nudity, sex, and pornography. "Children have access to too much too early," he thought to himself. Although he understood that censorship ran counter to the whole concept of the internet, he believed that certain sites were dangerous and should be banned for the public good.

Marcel long suspected that Clover had made contact with someone online. He called the lieutenant with his apprehensions about certain websites that might have had something to do with Clover's disappearance. He asked Lieutenant Freeman if the police were aware of all of the sites. He was confrontational when he spoke to the lieutenant, who defended the police by saying that they were well aware of the dangers posed by the internet, especially for adolescent girls and boys. He let Marcel know that the police already monitored many of the sites, but it was impossible to follow all of them.

Marcel worried that Clover had ventured off into one of the online teen communities and had met someone there, but the police had already done a thorough examination and forensic review of Clover's computers and there weren't any red flags. Marcel and the lieutenant discussed how easily children could be lured away from their homes by predators who exploited their weaknesses. Lieutenant Freeman agreed, and assured Marcel that the detectives were still checking to see if Clover had used another computer at school or at the town library. He told Marcel they were following the links and advised him to stay away from the site ads. The leads, the lieutenant said, were time consuming to follow and often led to dead ends. He let Marcel know that the police had confiscated Loralee's computer and were checking it for leads as well. The lieutenant suggested that Marcel leave the work to the techs in the department. After all, they were experts and it was their territory.

Marcel became more agitated and went to see Evelyn about his concern for Loralee's safety. His thinking was becoming more paranoid as time passed. Evelyn suggested that he take it easy. He habitually vented his concerns to her and repeated himself over and over again until she had to tell him as nicely as she could to ease off. "It's just that I'm so worried about Loralee," Marcel confided. "I don't want anything like what has happened to our Clover to happen to Loralee. Please talk to her again about the dangers of going on those teen sites. I've visited them trying to figure out what might have happened to Clover, and there are all kinds of predators out there just looking for innocent young girls like Clover and Loralee," he stated in a desperate tone to Evelyn. Marcel's mind was entertaining a host of dark thoughts.

"Thank you, Marcel." Evelyn gave him a well-needed hug and he softened for a moment, holding back tears. "We appreciate you sharing what you've learned about those sites with us. We'll definitely talk to Loralee as often as we feel is necessary. If you get any new leads about Clover, please call and let us know. Get some rest. You know that you, Hagatha, and Clover are always in our thoughts and prayers." After Evelyn walked with Marcel to the door, she and her husband spoke to Loralee again about the teen websites.

"I know, Mom. You don't have to drill me. It's overkill." They told Loralee that she was only allowed to email and text to people she knew—no strangers, no more visiting questionable sites and posting any photographs at all. "Take them all down!" Robert ordered.

"But Dad, certain sites can't be taken down; they stay forever."

Robert was furious. "I'll make a point of this at the next town meeting!" he exclaimed. "We must be able to do something . . . "

Loralee understood her father's arguments fully,

and agreed with them. She offered to give her cell phone to the police to trace her calls every month in case there were connections to the same people Clover knew. Lieutenant Freeman told Loralee that she could keep her phone, but to watch out for emails from people she didn't know, and to forward those messages to the police department right away.

Marcel kept in touch with Hagatha's parents, phoning them almost every day. He was grateful to the aunts, uncles, and cousins for their support, but he still felt helpless. The stress the grandparents experienced when trying to have a conversation with Hagatha and from listening to Marcel tell them about her condition caused them to become anxious and sick. She barely spoke, if she did at all. Marcel spared Hagatha, never discussing her parents' health with her or pressuring her to answer their calls. When they asked her how she was she would reply, "We're all fine. Clover will be home after school."

"One day at a time," he told them. "She doesn't talk to us in any meaningful way." "Why doesn't she speak?" Maura asked. "David and I don't understand . . . " "When she does speak, she tends to repeat the same thing over and over again," Marcel told them.

Marcel was concerned and listened to their health complaints, and was relieved when Hagatha's father and mother told him they had sought out alternative medical treatments. Her father's heart symptoms were improving using acupuncture and Reiki, and her mother's anxiety was helped by herbs and calming teas. "We finally listened to Hagatha's advice," her mother said, "and we're so glad we did—it's working!"

When Hagatha was well, she always tried to persuade her parents to use alternative medicine in addition to their doctors, and she and Clover had researched places they could go to be treated. Had Marcel told her, she would have been delighted to know that they'd finally followed her suggestions. Hagatha's father told Marcel how he regretted not listening to them both earlier. Ironically, as Hagatha experienced anxiety and profound depression, her parents' ailments and stress were alleviated using the alternative treatments that she had long recommended to them. Getting Hagatha to follow her own advice was virtually impossible.

With the passage of time, Hagatha no longer welcomed calls from her close neighbors Evelyn and Loralee, nor did she allow them inside her house anymore. Hagatha felt tormented by everyone.

Marcel was at his wit's end. After Hagatha had put up a royal fight, a social worker from the town who worked with the schools visited her. Never before in her practice had she ever encountered anyone as traumatized as Hagatha. The emptiness Hagatha felt within herself was overwhelming to her and to those around her. She couldn't respond to the social worker's attempts to engage her in the simplest of conversations, even conversations that centered on Clover. Her despondency grew and she carried it like a weight on her shoulders. Marcel tried his best to ease her suffering by cooking comforting meals for

her, like her favorite tuna casserole with green peas
and chocolate pudding, but that failed too. To his
dismay, she wouldn't even take a taste of the tuna
and ate only one spoonful of pudding. Her state of
mind was beginning to take a toll on her physically.
At least before, she would eat small portions, now it
was only a bite here and there.

Eventually, Marcel and Hagatha stopped speaking
to one another entirely. Each time Marcel
approached her to give her a hug she would extend
her arms as a buffer against him coming closer.
Marcel met and consulted with a well-known
psychologist who told him to give her "positive
feedback" whenever he could; but what she felt was
needed was for Hagatha to come in to be evaluated
for medication and therapy, perhaps staying in a
facility where she could be observed twenty-four
hours a day.

"Absolutely not," he bluntly said in a growing
rage. Marcel became infuriated at the very thought of
sending Hagatha to a mental facility. "Not my wife!"
he said. "That's for people who give up and I'm not
giving up!" As he stood up from his seat he scraped
the chair along the floor, nearly toppling over the
lamp behind him. Marcel refused both alternatives.
He didn't want to push Hagatha and thought that
backing off and allowing her space and time to heal
was best. "Hospital protocols," he muttered on his
way out the door, "everyone wants to take the easy
way out . . . pills masking what she must cope with.
My wife always comes first! Therapy would be

useless; she doesn't speak. We'll manage on our own!"

Sophia, Hagatha's caretaker, was a godsend through all the turmoil, but she didn't work every day of the week. Marcel knew months ago that Hagatha was unable to go back to teaching so he had filled out the necessary forms requesting a leave of absence. She was receiving checks for as long as the time period permitted. A holistic physician suggested herbs and teas to calm Hagatha while she healed, and that was acceptable to Marcel. Sophia was able to get her to drink the herbal teas and her demeanor seemed to improve.

There were, however, weekends when Marcel came home to find the kitchen torn apart. The cabinets and drawers were pulled open, the contents strewn all over the floor like a thief had broken in searching for things of value to steal. The refrigerator door was ajar, with its perishables left scattered over the counters and floor. Rancid food filled the sink. Marcel was never harsh or critical, but pulled himself together enough to clean up after his wife when Sophia wasn't there. When he attempted to ask Hagatha why she behaved the way she did, she would run out of the room and cower in a corner holding "Esther," the piece of blanket from Clover's childhood. He eventually learned to buy only non-perishable foods for her.

Marcel thought it best to leave Hagatha to her own thoughts, hoping that her anger and anxiety would lessen with time. She made it clear by her actions that Marcel was in the way. Without Sophia, Hagatha would have fallen apart completely months ago; coming into the household the few days she did during the week was enough to anchor her. Although her wide-eyed, expressionless face gave Hagatha the appearance of a person devoid of feeling, her actions told another story. She wasn't only depressed, she was angry.

Hagatha was lost in the vast empty space where Clover belonged. She thought she was to blame for Clover's disappearance. Every day that passed, a new memory appeared in her mind like an old movie replaying itself. From time to time, Marcel would catch her laughing as if someone had told her a joke, and then the laughter would stop, turning into tears or anger. He assumed she was reliving some vignette from the past, perhaps a pleasurable memory of Clover when she was younger. The weekends were the darkest days of the week for Hagatha because Sophia didn't work and Marcel had to pick up the slack. The small, quartered sandwiches of various kinds that Sophia made in advance were a saving grace. For Marcel, the weekends were nightmarish. Hagatha would call for Clover except for those times when she was quiet, lost in reverie of times past. It was then he would sit and look at his wife, wishing he could read her mind, and remembering her as she used to be.

Hagatha sat still on the couch, vividly recalling Clover's first birthday party. Earlier in the day she had been rummaging through her daughter's long outgrown party dresses. The smallest detail was sharp in her mind as she recalled Clover upstairs dressing in her party clothes with the help of Hagatha's mother and dad, while she set out the party plates and cups on the table. She glanced out of the corner of her eye at the pile of gifts in the dining room, boxes beautifully wrapped waiting for Clover. Bouquets of pink balloons tied with pink ribbons filled the room. ("Pink" was one of Clover's first words. Pronounced "pick," Clover would repeat the word as she gathered pink clover with her mother in the field next to the barn, grasping the stems so tightly in her little fists that they would break in half.) Grandma had made Clover's dress, an unforgettable pink dress made up of many layers of material with a ruffled, white petticoat underneath, and exquisite buttons she bought at a vintage store.

For a moment Hagatha's reverie was interrupted by the realization that Clover's talent for making clothing came as much from her own mother as herself. She didn't dwell on her mother, but quickly returned to scenes of Clover at her birthday party. She remembered Marcel taking photograph after photograph in Clover's room before the party began, until he ran out of film and had to dash out to the drugstore to buy more. Clover cried out after him, "Daddy, Daddy," as if to say, "Wait for me, Daddy, I want to go too!" But Grandma swept her up in her arms, kissing her face, and before long she had forgotten about her daddy. When Clover was ready, she pranced out of her room and held on to the banister as she and Grandma descended the stairs. Her curls were bouncing and her eyes gleamed as she ran to Mommy, who scooped her up into her arms. As Hagatha sat on the couch, she hugged her chest as if she were holding a one-year-old Clover to her bosom.

"Oh, my beautiful girl," she said. Clover's cheeks were flushed with excitement as she held on tight to her mother. Marcel returned with more film than he could possibly use and flashed one picture after another. She was a little girl who loved hugs, especially from both sets of grandparents. "Look, all your friends are here!" Hagatha exclaimed. Clover saw her playmates from her playgroup sitting at the table with their mothers behind them, some mothers smiling for the camera as Marcel made sure to film every single guest with his new video camera.

Hagatha put Clover at the head of the table with Grandma as she served the children their favorite all-beef hot dogs and turkey dogs, buttered corn on the cob, homemade chips, and cut-up strawberries, with apple juice. The highlight of the party was Grandpa dressed in a dog costume, barking as he handed out the hot dogs to all the giggling children. Hagatha chuckled to herself as the memory of her father's antics passed in front of her eyes.

Clover loved all-beef hot dogs smothered in relish on toasted rolls and cut into manageable bites. The mini cookies Marcel's mother made for Clover had clovers drawn on them with pink frosting, and were piled high on a beautiful French hand-painted plate set on the table. Marcel's parents had traveled from France to be at Clover's first birthday party. Among the many special toys they brought with them was a vintage tin merry-go-round with pink poodles—something no other child in the States would have—which Hagatha carefully put to the side for a time when Clover was older and could appreciate her gift. Finally, Hagatha came from the kitchen carrying Clover's favorite chocolate cake that she'd ordered from the bakery in town, made from a recipe that had been passed down for generations. The cake was made from scratch, with only the finest Belgian chocolate. Faith, the owner, had filled a separate container of their signature chocolate frosting for Hagatha and Clover to enjoy together on the side, more so for Clover though, who wore the chocolate smeared across her face and dress. Clover clapped her hands out of sheer happiness as one pink candle burned at the center of the cake.

Hagatha had ordered the same cake from the bakery for Clover's Sweet Sixteen Birthday Party, and Marcel's mother always sent Clover the same pink cookies in a tin from France that arrived two days before her actual birthday on the fifteenth. The cake for her sixteenth birthday was even more special, the frosting embellished with dogs made by a talented cake artist, sixteen of them with multi-colored collars with stars and pink fairies holding their leashes. Clover's grandmothers would stargaze with her when she was small, telling her stories about angels and stars that filled her young mind with wonder. Even when Clover was a teenager she said that she would never be too old to believe in fairies and angels.

As that thought flashed across Hagatha's mind, it brought her back to reality for a fraction of a second. There were cookies sitting on the counter waiting for Clover to come home. But what had happened to the birthday cake she'd ordered so many weeks ago? Marcel never told Hagatha he had called the bakery to cancel the order. At the time, they offered their help finding Clover. Although Marcel insisted on paying for the cake, there was no charge—Faith wouldn't take his money and generously offered to donate cakes for any fund-raising events they might hold for her. "We'll make Clover's cake again no charge the minute she comes home," Faith promised. "Just let me know."

For no particular reason, Hagatha recalled how much Clover loved dogs. Even as an infant, Clover crawled toward dogs in the park whenever one was in sight. As a toddler, Clover would run toward them fearlessly. The dogs were more afraid of her than she was of them!

Thinking about Clover's first birthday party had comforted Hagatha. She remembered Marcel taking pictures of the flowers on the table, an arrangement surrounded by pink clover that Hagatha ordered from the florist. If it hadn't been December she would've picked them herself.

Thinking about clover was another reminder of the day they picnicked surrounded by patches of crimson and pink clover. They decided on Clover's name at that time, and a bouquet of them became a tradition at all her birthdays. As she got older, Clover would say, "I'm my mom and dad's lucky clover!" Then she would laugh loudly and blow kisses at her parents, who in turn laughed equally as loud and blew kisses right back at her.

Referring to Clover, Hagatha would joke, "She's my extra special baby pink clover!"

Together, they would picnic behind the barn whenever the weather permitted. They'd sit on one of Clover's pink blankets that Hagatha had knit, looking through picture books spread out in front of them for Hagatha to read.

Clover was only four when she learned to read, surrounded by the carpet of yellow, blue, and purple wildflowers and the thousands of clovers that covered the ground. They would play and eat lunch.

Hagatha planted many more patches of various clovers, and watched them grow as she watched Clover grow up. Marcel knew that on any given afternoon he could find them doing homework in the yard or playing house in the barn.

Every time Marcel took Clover for walks in the park they were constantly interrupted, as she would always run to the dogs and try to pet them. He cherished those precious moments. Whenever he looked for greeting cards, he bought pictures of wildflowers in fields for his wife and daughter, writing notes inside that said, "To my beautiful girls—Forever, Dad."

Clover, like Hagatha, was very sentimental and kept every card her dad sent her from his travels. She also kept all the cards her mother made by hand. Hagatha would draw the pictures and write Clover special messages just for her in her own words. Over time Clover filled a drawer with their cards and intended to make them into a collage to hang on her wall one day. Marcel would pass by Clover's room and catch Hagatha reading the old cards with a wistful half-smile on her face.

Hagatha wasn't functioning and did little else besides reliving her memories over and over again. Other scenes would drift through her mind, like one of the most special days—when she and Marcel decided to name their baby "Clover." They were at the lake sitting on the old army blanket Hagatha's father had given her because it was too rough to sleep with but perfect for sitting on the grass outside. They had placed it in the wildflower patch full of crimson clovers, away from the sandy shoreline. Hagatha was already carrying extra weight, and she struggled to find a comfortable sitting position while Marcel poured two glasses of red wine. Taking a sip, they toasted their soon-to-be-born child and tasted the cheese and crackers they bought at the small delicatessen in town. The corned beef sandwiches that Leonard, the owner, made were the thickest Marcel had ever seen in all his travels. And there was always a side of extra pickles for Mrs. Baggard; Leonard assumed she craved pickles when in fact Hagatha had no such inclination. She finally had to tell Leonard that her real craving was for spaghetti with tomato sauce and big meatballs, topped by a mountain of Parmesan cheese. He laughed aloud and shook his head in disbelief. "No spaghetti here my dear, but for you I make," Leonard said in his slightly broken English, laced with a Yiddish accent. "Thanks, Leonard. We love your sandwiches. Our picnics wouldn't be the same without your special touch and besides, Marcel makes me spaghetti and meatballs at home whenever I ask."

"You have such a good husband, Mrs. B.," Leonard observed.

"Yes," I know," Hagatha proudly replied.

Whenever they sat on the grass there, Hagatha was always attracted by the wildflowers growing nearby and at the water's edge. She told Marcel that someday she would have the same kind of wildflowers planted at the entrance to their home.

"I'm so happy honey," she told Marcel, "Feel the beat of my heart." Then she reached down and drew his hand to just above her left breast and held it tightly in place so that he could feel the steady, strong beats of her heart against the palm of his hand.

"Yes," he replied. "Feel my heart beating too." Glancing at one another and grinning from ear to ear, they both placed their hands over Hagatha's bump. They could feel the baby move, and it connected the three of them as one unit, a complete family. It was an unforgettable moment of sheer happiness that they shared. They stood up to go down to the lake to fill Hagatha's Bali jar with water for the flowers; along the way, they picked buttercups, lavender, bunches of clover, and dandelions—some with fluffy white flowers and some without.

"You'll have your own garden of wildflowers soon, and loads of flowers to fill your blue jars," Marcel told her. "We should make a wish on the green clovers even if they don't have four leaves," Hagatha said. "C'mon, make a wish and we'll blow on the dandelions to seal it." Both of them wished, but believing the old tale about wishes not coming true if revealed, they kept them secret.

"Oh look, Marcel, here's a crop of dandelions that haven't gone to seed yet. I know, I'm going to make a bracelet out of them!" Hagatha stated excitedly, making the bracelet by intertwining dandelion stems with flowering clover.

Marcel made her a crown of clover for her hair. "You're my beautiful clover queen of the lake," he joked, "and this is our magical fairy tale kingdom." "Clover Kingdom," Hagatha added. They played like children in their little area of grass, although with their unborn baby onboard Hagatha was weighed down a bit. She was convinced by the way she was carrying the baby—low rather than higher up in her abdomen—that she would give birth to a baby girl. At least that was what friends, and even people passing by, told her.

Marcel would recite girls' names for fun, name

after name, but none of them interested Hagatha, who was playing with the clover and wildflowers. "Susie," "Elizabeth," "Lisa," "April," "Dawn," "Chelsea," "Violet"—none appealed to her. "Oh let's just have fun; the name will come to us later," she said. She took a handful of clover and playfully threw it at Marcel. He tossed some back at her in a battle. "Hagatha, wait! Stop!" he said as she continued showering him. "I've got it!"

"Got what?" she asked, giggling, still lording over her clover kingdom.

"I'm covered with clover," he said as Hagatha agreed.

"Yes, you are," she said, "and there's more to come!"

Hagatha took another handful and threw it high over Marcel's head so that the clover showered down like rain. She was tired and flopped down on the blanket to rest.

"It's right in front of our faces!" Marcel shouted loudly in happiness. He gathered bunches and bunches of clover from the grass and, leaning across her belly, he handed them to her. "Wait!" he exclaimed as he gathered more of the crimson flowers together, spreading them all over her. "Hagatha," he said, "guess!"

"Guess what?" she replied, giggling at his foolishness. "I'm covered!" He tossed them at her belly and laughed.

"It's right in front of our faces! See?" Marcel stood up and jumped up and down.

Hagatha looked at the beautiful flowers covering her and said, "Clover! Yes, that's what her name will be, Clover! Clover, of course!" Both of them sprinkled handfuls over each other until they were covered in them.

"Clover it is! It's a great name," Marcel said with finality in his voice, "yes it is, my love . . . Clover! She will grow to be beautiful, just like her mother and the wildflowers that grow here." They lay down and Marcel rolled in the beds of flowers, pleased with their decision. They kissed to seal the choice of their first child's name—Clover.

At that moment, a feeling of serenity came over them both. That same feeling of serenity was constant until their world was shattered by Clover's disappearance.

That day and Clover's first birthday reoccurred over and again in Hagatha's daydreams. They were cherished memories that were etched into her mind, reminding her of the happiness Clover brought into their lives from the time even before she was born. Following that day at the lake they went there every spring and summer. It became part of the treasured traditions and memories they made together. During these visits, they had picnics with their precious daughter in the wildflower field in their special spot, watching her as she sat on the edge of her favorite moss-covered rock by the lake picking the beautiful flowering crimson clover.

"It can't get any better than this," Marcel would say with pride after a day spent sitting among the wildflowers with his wife and child, enjoying Leonard's deli sandwiches and the meatballs Marcel had made that Hagatha and Clover loved so much.

****

One year of hell passed since Clover's disappearance, and then another. Days would go by when Hagatha wouldn't get out of Clover's bed. Her hair was messy and knotted. She hardly changed her clothes, which were the same ones she was wearing on the day Clover went missing. Only with Sophia's urging would she remove her uniform. There were unpleasant skirmishes whenever Marcel or Sophia tried to undress her to wash the clothing. Her hair was washed only after a battle with her husband, an ordeal he dreaded. On the day Sophia left for good, Hagatha screamed and yelled that she hated Marcel for taking her away. But so much money had been depleted in the continuing search for Clover that he simply had no choice.

After he had to let Sophia go, Marcel set aside times to clean the dust off the furniture and do the wash after he came home from work. Cutting back was a strain on Marcel. He had to argue with Hagatha to put on a fresh pair of Clover's pajamas so that he could wash the worn-out ones she continually wore at night to comfort her; she refused to part with them and he would have to wait for just the right moment. At the very least, he convinced her to watch while he washed and dried them as she stood to the side observing the process take place. Marcel assumed his wife had problems parting with Clover's favorite pajamas—the ones Clover wore before she changed into her school clothes on the day she went missing—because they held meaning for her, and that's why she wouldn't let them go. Hagatha always fought with Marcel in a tug-of-war until she gave in. She simply would not accept his help. She allowed herself to be vulnerable for only short spurts of time.

Marcel couldn't concentrate well at work anymore. He was always worrying and thinking he should be home with his depressed wife. However, he knew he had to keep his job and his sanity in order to pay the bills that poured in from hiring help and enlisting private detectives to work on Clover's case every day around the clock; thousands of dollars were being paid out. When he saw in black and white how much of their hard-earned money was coming out of their savings, Marcel stopped hiring detectives. He was a stressed man whose hobbies had long ago fallen by the wayside. He couldn't imagine spending time to relax. His youthful features grew older by the day. Marcel's friends and family urged him to take time off and go somewhere nearby for a vacation to relax, but there was no way he would go, not without Hagatha. He wouldn't go to his family in France even though they constantly begged him to come. "If only for a week to gather your thoughts," his mom would beg.

He usually went camping with Hagatha and

Clover at a certain time of year, sometimes just with Clover and other times with Clover and Loralee. The photograph of Clover on his desk, taken on one of their camping trips to bear country in Denver, haunted rather than comforted him.

Hagatha and her old teaching friends who had moved to Colorado would explore the art galleries and shops while he and Clover spent their time together in nature, becoming closer as they set up camp and roamed the woods. Clover loved sleeping in the tent inside her toasty down sleeping bag with her stuffed dog Sam, which almost always accompanied her on the trips. Hagatha avoided the woods saying, "The bugs belong on the flowers and trees, not on me. Also, I don't want to disturb the bears by being in the woods. I've heard that they can become quite grumpy when disturbed by people visiting. After all, who am I to disturb the wild animals? They deserve their peace and quiet as much as anyone does." Then she would put her hand over her mouth to hide her grin, wanting people to think she was truly serious about her statement. But the laughter that bubbled up from inside Hagatha always gave away her teasing.

The white rapids along the roads in Denver fascinated Clover, and she wondered if she would have the courage to ride the rapids someday. Marcel promised her that they would return for a vacation after she graduated from high school, bringing only Robert and Loralee this time because Hagatha and Evelyn didn't appreciate the wild terrain of bear country. Marcel would remark to Clover when she asked him why, "Well Clov, it's just not their cup of tea." He knew Hagatha wasn't comfortable in the wild at all.

Clover, on the other hand, was so excited about the prospect of white water rafting that she told her mother she'd get all the information they'd need to plan the trip. She and Loralee spoke about the trip whenever they were together. They proudly told their friends that they were going with their fathers to bear country to go white water rafting. The experience would be an opportunity for the girls to bond with their dads, and make special memories to take with them when they went off to college and for a long time afterward.

Marcel would say, "I promise to take you white water rafting Clover! I know I promised you a dog and I'm not breaking my promise, but I think going on this trip takes precedence."

"Well Dad, you know, in my book a dog comes first."

"It'll be a trip that none of us will ever forget, Clov." Marcel's own words reverberated inside his head whenever his eyes darted to the photograph, echoing Clover's loss like a single sound in an empty auditorium.

Marcel switched private detectives often to keep costs down, but after a while he couldn't continue paying what they were charging. They were so expensive that Marcel fired them one after another, finally keeping only one investigator part-time whose rates were reasonable. He suspected that they weren't doing their jobs anyway, but in truth, his suspicions were just an excuse for his frustration with the length of time that had passed without any progress. The investigator reported to Marcel every few months, but still there were no leads.

Marcel's thoughts were often preoccupied with Clover, rarely with what he was doing at the present moment. He was tormented thinking about his daughter every day, wondering where she was and if she were suffering some fate beyond terrible.

Hagatha began talking more and more to herself as she moved about the house, fixing Clover's favorite food as if her daughter were sitting there. Marcel thought that her preparing meals was at least doing something, even though when she served the food there was a place for Clover next to Hagatha at the table but none for him. Marcel sometimes felt that Hagatha blamed him for Clover's disappearance. He beat himself up by thinking that way. As time passed she appeared to be in a trance, totally blocking him and everyone else from her consideration. Every member of the family felt the sadness of losing both Clover and Hagatha, especially the person they once knew Hagatha to be.

Hagatha and Marcel's marriage was breaking up under the stress of Clover's absence. It was time for Marcel to leave and find a temporary place to live— maybe just a small room, not an apartment. He could not endure the pain of his wife's anger and utter rejection anymore. He couldn't watch his wife fall apart day after day. He rented a one-room studio, packed his two suitcases and left. Hagatha didn't confront or question him. The distance between them was becoming insurmountable. He could keep an eye on his wife by using his key and entering the house like a ghost. He doubted that she would even notice him or care. The decision was extremely difficult for him to make, yet Marcel was able to think more clearly since his move and he could assess Hagatha's often-strange behavior with clearer vision. Since he left, she had taken to sleeping on the floor of Clover's room. To be near Hagatha was a dead end for him; he was much better off being away.

He sought out friends and professionals again to help him answer his questions, however, the answers he received were all the same. They would say it was up to him, but what she needed was an inpatient program at a hospital for the mentally ill. Marcel couldn't conceive of Hagatha leaving their home to go to a facility for the mentally ill. He dreaded the thought. He didn't agree with the psychologists who said she was ill; rather, he believed that she couldn't yet cope with Clover's loss, nothing more. He insisted that she did not have a mental illness and that pumping her full of anti-depressants would interfere with her healing naturally and might even cause her to become suicidal. He believed her profound sadness was part of grieving, a natural— but unusually prolonged—process in Hagatha's case.

Marcel sought solace in his conversations with his

father, and they became even closer during this time. He found the courage to speak about his childhood relationship with him, a subject they never took the time to broach before. It took something as horrifying as Clover's disappearance to compel Marcel to discuss his innermost feelings as a child as he discussed Hagatha's behavior, which was as equally disconcerting as his feelings. Marcel told his father that as a child he was terrified of him because he was so strict, and before Clover's disappearance he often found him to be domineering and egotistical, but now, since they had been having conversations, he took comfort in his father's words and felt closer to him than ever before. Marcel finally had the humble and understanding father he had always wished for even as an adult.

Marcel arranged for Hagatha's meals and groceries to be delivered to her. Everyone in town knew the delivery boy from the grocery store, including Hagatha, who had watched him as he grew up. She wouldn't accept assistance from any family member when they came to visit, even though Marcel had asked her to accept their presence and the help they offered. They were met with a closed door or having the door shut in their faces without a word from Hagatha whenever they ventured over.

The neighbors who attempted to visit her from time to time reported back to Marcel about how she was doing, usually saying that she had said hello or goodbye through the closed door, nothing more. Marcel suspected that the only reason she said hello at all was to see if it was Clover on the other side of the door.

Hagatha's habit was to leave the kitchen door unlocked for Clover in case she lost her key. The neighbors would sometimes use the open back door to check on Hagatha, carefully entering so that they wouldn't be seen. It was convenient for the delivery boy, who put her meals on the table. Although he was timid at first, he was able to open the door and walk right in, put away the groceries in the cabinets and refrigerator, and observe Hagatha for Marcel without intruding. He emailed Marcel at work about what he observed and often wrote that she would pass him in the kitchen staring right through him as if he didn't exist. Evelyn visited almost daily to check on Hagatha, who would be sitting in a chair in Clover's room rocking back and forth without speaking for two to three hours. While Evelyn was visiting, she mostly averted her eyes as she twisted strands of her hair, but occasionally stared at Evelyn with a quizzical expression on her face as if she were going to ask her a question.

After a short time even Evelyn stopped coming over so often because she felt it was too depressing. Her feelings were crushed by Hagatha's anger toward her, which seemed to come in fits and starts. Hagatha would scream at her and it broke Evelyn's heart, taking a toll on her as well as her family. Robert offered to check on Hagatha and bring her what she might need, giving Evelyn a break from her odd behavior, but the first time he slipped into the house she saw him in the kitchen and, feeling intimidated, bolted as fast as she could up the stairs to barricade herself in Clover's room. Loralee still had difficulty accepting the loss of her friend and never slept without the stuffed dog, Sam. Whenever she went to visit, Hagatha would give her a quick hug, but when she realized that it was Loralee and not Clover, she pushed her away. Even Loralee began to feel rejected.

Hagatha was angry during the moments she wasn't depressed, and was either belligerent or unresponsive to everyone. She was able to live alone, but she was no longer the sweet teacher with the pretty smile whose friends enjoyed being around her. Her sadness had changed her into another person, and there seemed to be little prospect of her changing back to her former self.

One late afternoon, the neighbors heard crashing and loud yelling coming from the Baggards' home. They thought that the house had been invaded by a stranger, but it was Hagatha battling her demons. Items were raining out the front door onto the porch and walkway. Neighbors raced up the stairway, taking two steps at a time until they reached the top. Hagatha was on the front porch ranting, "Me, why didn't you take me instead? Where's my baby? Bring her back!" She spewed out a vile string of curse words. Her hair was wild and matted and her clothes were soiled. She lunged and drove herself against the wall of the house. She shattered the glass she was holding in her hand against the railing, and there was silence for a moment. Her neighbor Kevin, a retired fireman, ran to her. He watched as blood trickled from a shallow slit to her wrist dangerously close to a vein. Hagatha's face was contorted with pain for a moment when she saw the cut.

She resumed screaming, "Why? Why? What can I do to bring her back?" She was shaking her fist at the sky. The blood dripped in four separate rivulets across her forearm as she raised her arms in the air. Kevin positioned himself behind Hagatha and held her twisting and turning body still. Evelyn rushed up the steps as fast as she could and stood with the other neighbors, watching as Hagatha dropped to the floor, weak and weeping. Kevin's eyes welled with tears as he held her tightly.

Evelyn told Kevin, "I'll handle Hagatha!" She cradled her in her arms, rocking gently.

Kevin asked, "You're sure you can take care of her, Ev? Her wrist needs to be cleaned and wrapped."

Evelyn nodded, and Kevin stepped back.

"Call me if you need me," he said.

"Of course," Evelyn replied.

Hagatha's blood had stained her dirty clothing, along with what Kevin and Evelyn were wearing. She was soothed by Evelyn's touch much like a child is comforted by a mother's caress. Evelyn helped her stand and walk, brushing away a shard of glass with her shoe. She put her arm around Hagatha's tiny waist and guided her into the house and up to the third floor bathroom to clean and bandage her wrist, making sure that there were no slivers of glass. The neighbors couldn't help noticing the torn photographs of Hagatha on the floor of the front foyer, ripped up as if she wished to destroy herself.

One of the neighbors, Jill, stayed out of the way and made two cups of steaming hot tea for Hagatha and Evelyn while the others swept up the broken glass outside and wiped the blood from the porch floor and inside the hallway. They were at a loss about what to do for her. Jill, who had two teenaged daughters of her own, felt Hagatha's pain. Although she wasn't as close to Hagatha as Evelyn was, her daughters knew Clover well. Her torrent of anger had taken them by surprise. It was so unexpected coming now, after Clover had been missing for years.

In Hagatha's mind, her daughter's disappearance had just occurred. It was fresh in her mind every day of her life.

Evelyn thanked Jill and the other neighbors as they left, assuring them that she was able to handle the situation. She asked them not to tell anyone what had just happened and they all agreed to keep it hush-hush; no one was notified of Hagatha's tantrum out of fear that she might be taken away. That would have driven Marcel to distraction.

After a few hours of sitting together with her friend, Hagatha ate a bowl of soup so greedily she appeared to be starving. She lay down on the living room sofa next to Evelyn; she was calm with her there. And as harrowing as her outburst was, Evelyn viewed it as a necessary expression of Hagatha's profound and prolonged grief. She had held it in for too long. She thought that perhaps with enough outbursts Hagatha would help move herself beyond the overwhelming sorrow she felt. When Evelyn felt it was time to leave, Hagatha was peacefully falling asleep with Clover's blanket pulled up under her chin. She left one light on in the hallway and another in the bathroom. It was dark and late when Evelyn finally headed home.

CHAPTER 6

MARCEL'S TWO FAVORITE GIRLS

That night, Hagatha awoke with the glow of a soft light behind her. Something had roused her out of a sound sleep, but what? She walked down the hallway and directly into the dark front sitting room, making her feel disoriented. There wasn't any light filtering through the windows, just darkness. There was no moonlight, no stars to gaze upon, and no Evelyn to comfort her.

Then she had a sense that Clover was speaking to her. She could hear her voice, but only inside her head, begging her to come: "Mom, I'm here! Please come, please!"

"Where? Where baby?" Hagatha spun around in a circle. And then Clover's voice faded away. Hagatha clutched her wrist. She felt the cut throbbing, a reminder of the afternoon and the pain of reality.

Marcel missed his two favorite girls. He carried that weight on his shoulders every night as he lay in his claustrophobic room with stark white walls. As difficult as it was to focus, he worked seven days every week, sometimes during the evenings, to keep busy so that he wouldn't think about them all the time. The nights alone without Hagatha were hellish. He phoned her several times throughout the day to leave "I love and miss you" messages, and at nighttime he would say, "Sweet dreams to my girls."

Hagatha would listen to them and as he was speaking she felt his absence. He would clear all the messages when he came by to make sure there was enough space to leave more. His parents and Hagatha's gave up calling the house (even though Marcel had asked them to call his cell phone if they wanted to talk). They then called him at work because when Hagatha picked up the receiver and listened for a voice, she wouldn't speak unless, they assumed, it was Clover's voice she heard.

His co-workers told him again and again to take a break, but Marcel didn't want time to dwell on his daughter and wife so he took on even more assignments. He was exhausted, and it showed. He worked harder to keep busy. On the weekends, when he worked only half-days, he would drive to Clover's school and morbidly retrace her steps home. No one ever noticed him. He was like an invisible man, even more so as the emptiness that he felt on the inside also seemed to show on the outside. At times, he parked in front of the house and would sit staring at his home without going inside. The neighbors were the only ones who noticed him then, watching from the opened curtains of their adjacent homes. Sometimes while Marcel was keeping vigil outside his home, they would suddenly appear on his doorstep with casseroles for Hagatha. He was so grateful for their kindness that he wrote thank-you notes to all of them.

The memory of Clover's laugh rang in his ears and his tears flowed whenever he entered his home. Marcel created a blog to enlighten parents about sites that posed threats to children and teens, and made notes for schools to be alert to these dangerous sites. Maintaining people's awareness became his passion. He couldn't believe how quickly the years passed, and still there wasn't any information about Clover's disappearance.

Marcel mused about his Hagatha, whom he loved fiercely, picturing their wedding day. She was so pretty and he was so proud. He had to repeatedly convince himself that leaving the family house was best for both of them despite his vows never to leave her, to be with her "for better or for worse, in sickness and in health."

Each time he walked through the door of their house he felt like another piece of his heart was being torn out. The wedding picture that hung in the hallway reminded him of every moment before and during their wedding day. He recalled the times before they were married, particularly the day they discussed how life would be as they grew older together. He said, "We'll take out our teeth and dip our muffins in tea."

Then Hagatha wryly added, "Speak for yourself! Maybe you'll remove your teeth, but mine will be intact," as she and Marcel laughed together.

Then Marcel said, "I will hold your hand forever and walk with you through the clover patches and wildflowers until the end of the world." How they used to laugh!

He yearned to walk along the lake with her again. He wrote cards that he left on the kitchen table, inviting Hagatha to have a picnic with him when the weather turned warm. He remembered that she always carried a basket packed with his favorite tuna sandwiches that she'd made especially for him with chopped celery and onions, and—at his special request—she added grape jam. There were fresh strawberries for dessert, and after they finished eating they would throw crusts of bread at the gaggles of squawking geese. Marcel recalled the afternoon a small flock of geese chased after him to take the bag of crusts for themselves, and one of the geese bit his ankle, sending Hagatha into a fit of laughter.

Hagatha always carried mints with her and never failed to offer Marcel one after he finished eating, especially when he had eaten onions. In those days, they kissed more often than most couples, and would always seal their picnics with a romantic kiss and a joke or two. Marcel remembered countless times they'd gone to the movies and shared buckets of popcorn, shoveling handfuls into their mouths, most of it falling onto their chests and into their laps.

It seemed so much had changed. Now it would never occur to Hagatha to share a piece of bread with him. She didn't have a word to say. Marcel berated himself for them not having a second child, a companion for Clover and an anchor for Hagatha.

He considered getting a dog like the one they were about to get for Clover, a dog from the rescue that would be a companion to Hagatha. But then he reconsidered, thinking that she could barely take care of herself. Now was not the right time. Marcel wondered if a time would come when she could look in the mirror and see herself again. "Will she ever understand that she's missed as much as Clover?" he asked himself. "Will she ever realize how loved she is?"

Clover hadn't come home. She was among the vast number of missing children, yet Marcel and Hagatha both believed she would return one day. During one of his visits, in a moment of desperation, Marcel asked her, "But what about us? We've disappeared as well."

Hagatha shrugged her shoulders and in a flat tone of voice answered with a terse, "Okay." This saddened him even more—that wasn't an answer.

Another time when he came to visit, he told her, "You know, Hagatha, we were so close. What's happened to us? Can we take a walk or try to have a conversation, please? We should be closer, not farther apart. Please, hear me out . . . "

Hagatha, who was sitting by one of the living

room windows overlooking the street, peeked out the narrow space between the blinds and replied, "Soon, I guess." She had been listening, but her heart was still closed. At least her reply gave Marcel a bit of hope.

His mind took him back to their wedding day, just the two of them, and how Hagatha looked wearing a simple white gown with her mother's veil and carrying her grandmother's clutch bag. She wore vintage pearls—such a beautiful necklace, with a diamond broach on the clasp holding the precious pearls together. It was a gift from her great-grandmother. The family assumed that Clover would be next to wear the pearl necklace on her wedding day.

Marcel envisioned Hagatha as she began walking toward him to take their wedding vows. He was awed by her beauty and overcome with love. His parents adored Hagatha. They wanted the newly married couple to move to France to be close to them, but she couldn't bear leaving the job she loved so much or moving further away from her own parents. Since Marcel traveled because of his job, making trips to France fit easily enough into his routine.

Marcel recalled the moment before Hagatha walked down the aisle, when complete silence fell upon the room. Marcel turned to Bradley, his best man and roommate at BU, and whispered, "Look at her. She is so beautiful that her radiance could light up the sky."

"I hear you," he replied.

"Isn't she something?" Marcel asked. "Yes, you're one lucky guy. Just don't trip over yourself like the day the both of you went on your first date." "I won't," Marcel assured him. A few more minutes and Hagatha and Marcel would be joined for life. He could hardly wait. He reveled in these memories of beauty and joy despite his grief. "I must keep these memories alive to see me through the bad times," he thought. "I must keep the faith for my girls." There were many nights Marcel phoned Bradley to help him hold it together. Bradley stuck by his friend and was always there for him, coming to his aid when Clover first went missing to help search for her. He mailed cards to Hagatha to keep her spirits up.

More time was passing by, and Marcel's job now took him out of the country for longer periods. He made sure Hagatha had everything she needed. Neighbors told him that his wife was taking walks lately, circling around the house and barn, and sometimes venturing outside their property to look at Loralee's house from the long driveway that led to the front entrance, then around the corner walking across the neighbors' lawns. When Marcel learned about his wife's walks he was wary, and hesitant to be optimistic, but at least he was encouraged by her wish to go outside in the fresh air. Although he was curious about where she was going, he didn't want to impose by asking them to follow her; but he did ask them to let him know if the house lights didn't go on in the evening

Marcel hadn't hired any private detectives for quite a while. It had been years since Clover vanished, and to him a lifetime had passed, though little had changed. Time virtually stood still at the Baggard home. Evelyn tried to be uplifting, telling Marcel how positive Hagatha's walks were, and he echoed her optimism about Hagatha's new habit. Evelyn, and especially Marcel, passed along this positive attitude to his family. There was seemingly further reason to be optimistic when the delivery boy mentioned that one time he went into the kitchen and Hagatha had been eating ginger cookies; she offered some to him . . . and to the empty chair where Clover used to sit. Despite her odd behavior, Marcel was encouraged by her eating cookies— maybe, he thought, she'd put some weight back on her too-slender body. Clover especially loved ginger cookies and Hagatha was reminded of her daughter whenever she ate them.

Every spring Marcel hired gardeners to tend to the overgrown lawn and flowers, making sure it looked as it always had in order to please Hagatha, even though he wasn't sure that she could appreciate the beauty of the gardens anymore. Her existence revolved around her long-lost daughter. She was tethered to her daughter: physically, emotionally, and spiritually—her daughter was part of her soul.

When Hagatha allowed Marcel to kiss her cheek, he noticed that her face was no longer soft; her complexion was dry and pale despite the sun that fell on her during her walks and when she would sit on the porch. He found the jar of her favorite face cream on her dresser, opened it, and saw that there was barely any left. Marcel guessed the jar looked the same way the last time Hagatha had used it years ago when Clover first went missing. "I could buy the same cream at the drugstore," he thought, as she sat in kitchen and he dabbed what was left of the sweet-smelling lemon cream on her face and lovingly applied it. He told her, "I'm so glad you're taking walks now, my dear. The fresh air will lift your spirits." Hagatha nodded her head with a crooked frown on her face.

Then she off-handedly said, "I'm walking to meet Clover. I don't want to miss her when she gets out of school."

"Yes, I understand," he replied. His heart was suddenly troubled—he wished that he could take comfort in his wife's arms and cry. Marcel realized his wife had not been living in reality for years, and still existed in a distorted reality—a make-believe place in her head. Yet, after all this time, he believed she could have a breakthrough. He wondered if the time had come for her to talk to someone professional. He now understood that Hagatha's walks weren't a sign of improvement after all, they were irrational ventures out of the house to find Clover.

He knew it was time to call her family to ask for their opinions. After sitting and pondering his wife's condition, he concluded, "No, not my Hagatha— eventually she'll return to herself on her own terms.

I'll wait." His love and belief in her were the foundation of his hope. His late night conversations with his father helped him to hold on to his convictions. He advised his son to speak to his mother, who would know better about dealing with Hagatha.

Marcel called his mom the next day to hear whatever advice she might have, particularly because she was a woman. Her suggestion was for him to follow his heart. "Hagatha is your wife and you love her," she said, "and this is not the time for textbook logic."

"Yes, Mom," he answered, "that's exactly what Dad said." His mother's advice rang true. When he prayed to Clover he felt more at peace. The continual up-and-down ride of losing hope in Hagatha's recovery and then believing again tired him, though he never doubted that Clover could hear his pleas.

Marcel neatened the kitchen table after Hagatha when he visited and always looked in the cabinets and refrigerator in case she might need certain foods she liked to eat. Lately, things were in order. It appeared she was eating oatmeal and drinking milk to the exclusion of all other foods, which he had to throw away. Ginger cookies were always on her list of foods to buy. It was apparent that she had only been using Clover's bedroom, where the bed was unmade and tousled from her sleeping there. The rest of the house was perfectly neat. It was time for Marcel to end his visit with Hagatha. Leaving her at seven gave him enough time to eat his dinner and go to sleep at his own place. He felt like he was a guest in his own home, a place where time stood still. He was more comfortable in the rooming house. He wasn't getting through to her, just like all the other times. He had refused to respond to her remark about meeting Clover after school beyond what he'd already said—it was better left alone.

The following weekend he stayed over and slept in the sitting room. When he was about to leave, he told her, "I'm going away on a long trip in a day or two, Hagatha. I'll be away for a month or so." When he announced that he was going on this long trip, she hardly acknowledged him, although she did walk to the front door as if she were preparing to say goodbye. Hagatha stood at the door staring at her husband. He returned her stare with greater intensity.

He whispered, "I love you with all my heart," then kissed her forehead. "Do you understand me?" he asked insistently. She blinked and shook her head yes. She held her slender fingers out to him and Marcel took her hand. "Oh Hagatha, I love you dearly." Marcel dropped to his knees. "Please take care. I'll be back to see you the moment this trip ends. Everyone is at your disposal, my dear." She squeezed his hand and then let go. Marcel stood up. He knew she understood and he felt that there still might be a ray of hope.

Evelyn had offered to check on Hagatha every other day, and he made sure to give her an emergency telephone number in case Hagatha needed him. He let her know that Hagatha seemed to be making some progress lately by saying a few extra words, and he couldn't thank her enough for her help. "Your friendship means a great deal to me," he told her, "and even more to Hagatha." "Don't you worry, we'll be just fine!" Evelyn replied.

Marcel believed that Evelyn was the best company for Hagatha. She never stopped believing in her, and was in awe of her dogged determination to find Clover. Loralee visited on Saturdays from college. She knew that her mother hadn't given up all hope and neither had she. The three of them, Evelyn, Loralee, and Hagatha, would occasionally walk together outside, with Loralee telling Hagatha stories about school, attempting to engage her in conversation, usually unsuccessfully. Hagatha would respond by hurrying into the house and running upstairs to Clover's room. Robert would reassure his daughter that sticking by Hagatha was the right thing to do even though so much time had elapsed since Clover's disappearance.

Marcel mentioned to Evelyn that Hagatha had been writing in a diary, a book embossed with beautiful autumnal colors that was meant as a present for Clover's birthday. "She's been very secretive about it," he told her. "If you see it let me know." "Yes, of course I will. It certainly would be helpful to know what goes on inside that head of hers."

The last thing Marcel did before leaving town was

to go to Faith's bakery, where he used to buy chocolate cakes and candy for Hagatha and Clover; "something special for his special girls," he would say. Without Marcel saying a word, Faith selected Hagatha and Clover's favorite chocolates—raspberry and caramel fillings in dark chocolate—and wrapped them in boxes tied with blue ribbon. Marcel thanked her, and on his way home bought a bunch of pink clover at a shop that sold wildflowers. When he returned to the house, Hagatha was sitting at the kitchen table among small piles of paper she had cut and was piecing together into a collage. He said good-bye to her again, but when he held her close he felt like there was a hollow person in his arms, limp, without spirit. He placed the beautifully wrapped boxes of chocolates on the kitchen table next to the bouquet. To entice her, Marcel opened the box meant for her and left it there with its cover off, leaving Clover's untouched. Marcel was on his way out, looking back one more time before closing the door. He was wishing for some kind of response from his wife, anything—a gesture or remark. Apathetic, Hagatha stood there staring at the chocolates and flowers. There was nothing said between them. As he was closing the door, he glanced at her once more; she had pulled a stem from the bunch and clenched the clover in her hand smelling the fresh fragrance of the tiny pinkish petals. She looked at her box of chocolates. Then, Hagatha turned and stared at her husband and the slightest of smiles began to cross her face in appreciation of his thoughtfulness. Marcel was delighted and left with a touch more hope. He allowed himself a brief smile as his heart jumped. "Yes!" he said to himself. "She feels our love still. Her love has been buried underneath the weight of her grief. Someday, my wife and daughter will return to me . . . someday . . ."

CHAPTER 7

DAILY WALKS

It had been four years since Clover went missing. Even though time was passing by, Hagatha's emotions were still unstable. The people in town whispered that Clover was gone for good and some would tell Evelyn that at this point they believed she was not ever coming back. There were dark rumors that she'd been kidnapped by someone who had seen her photograph on the computer, the one taken that day at the barn store—maybe someone had become obsessed with her and she was taken away to a place it was impossible to escape from, or worse yet, she was being held by slave traders. Then, even more heinous, was the possibility that she could be dead.

Among the neighbors, only Loralee and her family believed without a doubt that she would come back someday. Dark imaginings—they were easy for folks to conjure up and leave to fester. Loralee discovered notes Hagatha had written to Clover that said in one way or another that she was waiting for her and could feel her presence every day. When Loralee informed Marcel, he set up a meeting for a renowned psychic to come to the house and speak to Hagatha. They exchanged a few words, and then Hagatha announced that the woman couldn't tell her anything she didn't already know. "My baby is out there," she said, "I know it's true." The psychic encouraged her not to give up, and told Marcel she felt a strong spirit in the house and that she believed that Clover's presence was still on earth. Marcel was torn between what was rational and what he also felt to be true, but in spite of his ambivalence, in the end he took the psychic's words to heart. Hagatha declared, "Clover is right here with me, I can feel her!" The psychic took Marcel aside and said in confidence that it was possible that Clover's spirit was so strong that it might seem as if she were actually present in the house with them, and that accounted for Hagatha's saying that Clover was with her. Marcel nodded his head.

Clover's disappearance was still a topic of conversation among Loralee and Clover's old school friends. They had all graduated from high school; some went on to college while others were working. Loralee would argue with them, insisting that Clover would be coming home one day, and they all said she was foolish. They accused her of being as crazy as Mrs. Baggard. Loralee insisted it was true, and that she heard from her mom that the psychic said that Clover could still be out there. Some neighbors pitied Hagatha because she was disheveled and alone, while others understood that in addition to being alone she was deeply depressed and living as best she could. Most were incapable of placing themselves in her situation and empathizing with such profound sorrow. There were a few who said that they wouldn't want to go on living if they were in Hagatha's shoes. But Hagatha wasn't aware of others' opinions.

Marcel continued hanging flyers on the trees in Emerson and in surrounding towns, and cities even further away, having exhausted every other method of locating Clover. The flyers had to be taken down; they were ripped and faded from the weather, some almost illegible. Marcel would replace them as often as he could, never relinquishing hope that someday she would be seen. At one time the flyers provoked interest among parents—even paranoia—but that time had long passed. The fact that so much time had passed wasn't a good sign for Clover, and although the townspeople did take precautions for a few years, they no longer wondered if their own children were vulnerable—there had been no other incidents of missing children in their town and eventually they began to forget about Clover. At town meetings the people didn't mention what happened to her as often as they once had. Many of them didn't believe that the same thing could happen to their own children. Others were convinced she had run away with a boy she'd met from another town or online. After Clover's disappearance, the schools' principals initiated a program to raise the younger children's awareness of how to prevent abductions, taught by experts and children who had experienced an attempted kidnapping or assault as a result of meeting strangers on the internet or on the street on their way to and from school. Computers in the schools could be used for research and homework only. At parent-teacher meetings, the teachers advised parents to monitor their children's internet use, but over time the parents were less vigilant despite Marcel's efforts to raise their awareness by speaking about online threats at PTA meetings.

Hagatha's students graduated from the elementary school where she had taught, and some of her fellow teachers moved on to other jobs in the school system and other teachers replaced them. The world had changed and so had the town. Things were not the same as they used to be when Hagatha was a teacher, and now she was almost unrecognizable to her friends and neighbors alike. The few teachers who remained in their positions for years knew Hagatha, but said little to each other about her life, not wanting to add to rumors that had been spread about her for years. The police kept in touch with Marcel from time to time, preferring to call him on his cell phone so that Hagatha wouldn't be alarmed.

Hagatha became more eccentric. After being alone in her house with the windows closed for so long, the air took on a distinctive, musty odor inside. Walking outside was one way to avoid the acrid smell, although she was oblivious—it was Marcel who noticed the stuffiness now when he came into the house. He aired out all of the rooms. One of Hagatha's new routines over the past year was to visit the elementary school where she once taught, carrying her daughter's old backpack and a basket to pick up loose trash. She would give incoherent, rambling speeches to the children warning them about the dangers of talking to strangers and texting pictures to posted sites. Her ranting and bizarre behavior frightened some of the younger children, while the older ones taunted her. When pink clover was in season she would offer handfuls, but they refused to accept the flowers, thinking Hagatha appeared too dirty, an odd character who spoke in an eerie way. One of the bullies once tore them out of her hands, where they fell to the ground and he stomped on them. Hagatha's sorrowful moan frightened some of the children while others laughed. She bent down and picked them up, one by one, not leaving a single flower behind, and put them in her basket. The rank odor of her body repelled them, and they said that she picked the flowers just to smell better. They viewed her as an old lady who was crazy, the subject of their schoolyard ridicule—a bag lady, a woman everyone would've rather overlooked as they passed by. The faculty members who noticed her at school viewed her as a sad soul and let her be. The principal knew her and considered her to be harmless. He allowed her to do as she wished despite her appearance—

she'd had enough hurt in her life, he thought.

Hagatha collected cans and bottles from rummaging in the trash, all the while searching for clues to Clover's disappearance. The children were too young to know about the tragedy in her life. They saw a filthy, ragged woman who was dressed in a heavy coat even though the weather was warm and carrying a basket filled with trash. They laughed at her and said she was a dirty bag lady. Some children were so cruel they threw fruit and pebbles at her and mimicked the way she walked. Hagatha wouldn't respond angrily to her tormenters; she understood that they were children who didn't know better and needed to learn. Bullies in the schoolyard were so vulgar they shocked the other children with the names that spewed out of their mouths. Some children would take her picture with their cell phones. Luckily, they were caught by one of the teachers who had them remove the photographs before they got into trouble by posting their shots to other children or putting it live on the internet. Hagatha was oblivious to what the children were doing; she certainly hadn't kept up with the fast pace of technological change.

At recess, one of the children said he thought he knew her name from an older kid who went to high school. They found out her name was indeed Hagatha Baggard. Now she wasn't simply a bag lady, but was nicknamed "Haggy Baggy the Bag Lady" by the kids who saw her on her daily walks. She would repeatedly tell them to be careful and to beware of strangers. They didn't take her warnings seriously and the name-calling became worse by the day. They believed she was merely a crazy lady with a funny name.

Day after day Hagatha withstood their verbal abuse. One of the older children once lunged at her and pulled at her basket, trying to take it away from her. Hagatha fought back, clenching the handle so tightly her knuckles turned white, and in spite of her frailty she managed to keep it. The bullies persisted in tormenting her, pulling at her clothes, trying to rip them. At the same time, another bully approached her from the rear, attempting to grab Clover's backpack off her shoulders. She fell backward onto the ground, just missing hitting her head on the pavement. Hagatha became enraged and screamed at the boy with such ferocity he was rendered speechless, frightened by the harshness of her voice. He ran away. She'd hurt her neck, but ignored the pain. He ran off calling her a hag and a witch. These objects had belonged to Clover and held a great deal of meaning for Hagatha, who wasn't averse to defending herself from the children's attacks on them.

Whenever the teachers were able to catch the children harassing Hagatha, they would be sent to detention immediately. The administration met with the teachers to try to put an end to these confrontations. Principal Walker considered disciplining the children even further by suspending them for several days at a time if they touched her in an aggressive way again. He was in the position to educate the children and he called for classroom meetings. He explained that Hagatha was a human being who deserved respect despite the way she looked. The principal didn't want to involve the police and take the chance of the encounter becoming public. The bullies' belligerence eased somewhat with the threat of suspension hanging over their heads, and having to deal with their parents. He suspended several students who crossed way beyond the line when they ganged up and threw a rotten apple in Hagatha's face. Her cheek was so hot and swollen that she ran home and applied ice to her face and didn't return to school for a few days. Their parents complained to the principal about allowing a bag lady on school premises and threatened to take the matter to the school committee, but Principal Walker maintained his stance and told them plainly that there was a zero tolerance policy for bullying at the school no matter who the target of the bullying was. The majority of parents were supportive.

Still, many of the bullies muttered derogatory names and tossed rotten tomatoes at Hagatha any chance they had. They would hide, and then seemingly come out of nowhere and throw the tomatoes at her, which left her covered with the meat and juice of the tomatoes that burst into a soggy mess. Hagatha, although unsettling to some people, was within her rights to walk near the school without becoming the target of the children's derision.

At home, after suffering the children's abuse, Hagatha would sit on Clover's bed, making sure she was on the side where Clover used to sleep to feel closer to her and more secure. She spoke to Clover, telling her what had happened in the playground and that she understood how children were. She would wipe off whatever the children had thrown from Clover's backpack and sling it over the chair next to the bed, never far from her reach. The diary that piqued Marcel's curiosity was tucked furtively inside the book bag where, she believed, no one would find it—it was only for her own eyes to see.

Her daily ritual was to take Clover's clothes out of the dresser drawers, unfold them, then fold them again and place the small piles back in perfect order, just as they were when Clover put them there. She would speak sweetly to each item, as if she were expecting a response. The top drawer was a collection of mismatched belongings from the time Clover was young until she was fifteen. Hagatha would pick up each piece, study it as she recalled its significance, and return the object to the exact spot where it had been. Clover loved collecting old beads and broken jewelry, sea glass and dried flowers. She told her mom that one day she would use them to create her own line of fashion jewelry. She said she was planning to make special, one-of-a-kind boxes embellished with the same odds and ends, each having its own significance, and decorate mirrors and furniture with them. Clover collected pretty little pieces just like Hagatha, who had her own collections of vintage items displayed throughout her house, from furniture to miniature teddy bears no more than two inches high.

Clover's fascination with collecting began when she was five years old with her collection of flying pigs, small china figures of elephants and fairies, and anything with a clover on it. As Hagatha gazed at the shelves above Clover's vanity, she remembered Clover asking her father if pigs could really fly. When Marcel told her they couldn't, she asked, "Then why do they have wings?" and "Why do grown-ups say 'when pigs can fly' all the time?" Neither mom nor dad had an answer for her. They set their minds to finding an answer Clover would be able to understand. Finally, Hagatha told Clover that the company that made the pigs thought the idea of flying pigs was cute because of the saying "when pigs fly," which meant that if pigs could fly, then anything was possible. She said, "Clover, if your daddy could change into a dog with wings and fly, then anything is possible." Clover tilted her head to the side and giggled at Hagatha's attempt to draw a comparison that went beyond her understanding. She didn't grasp the meaning and simply shrugged her shoulders, saying "Well, that's not possible unless Daddy put on a costume with wings, and then he still couldn't fly. Besides, Daddy can't be a dog, and even if he could, he wouldn't have wings. That's silly, Mommy." She understood that somehow the wings were special and that was enough to satisfy her curiosity. "You'll understand when you're older," Hagatha said. Clover asked about the flying pigs each time Marcel would bring her one from his travels. Even later on, "when pigs fly" eluded her—it was not until around her thirteenth birthday that it made total sense to her. "You know, Daddy," she said, "pigs never could fly—it's just a saying—so that if they did fly, that would mean that anything is possible." "Yes, sweetheart, it's a conundrum, isn't it? But you understand." Clover's facial expression became quizzical as she asked, "Daddy, what's a conundrum?" "We'd best look that up in the dictionary," he said.

Clover's grandpa in France sent her a set of five china elephants ranging in height from the largest male to a baby, perfect for playing house. Fairies and angels lit her imagination and she would make up stories about them sleeping inside the wildflowers in the fields until nighttime, when they would come alive and ride on the elephants. When the cold weather arrived, she envisioned the fairies bringing the clover seeds into her room and hiding them until spring when the fairies would take flight and plant them in the earth. Clover's fairies would appear only when she was alone, she told her mother. "There are so many of them," she explained. "And they don't talk to grown-ups."

"I see," Hagatha would say. The fairies were safe in the fields when it was warm, and when they were tired they rode on the passing butterflies. They even had names. Hagatha loved hearing Clover's fairytale fantasies. Clover's favorite fairy hung from a hook up in one of the corners of her room, an all-pink fairy dressed in layers of sheer material that trailed behind her. She carried a basket of white roses. It was a one-of-a-kind fairy that Marcel couldn't resist buying for Clover when he was in Paris and passed by a shop that sold only fairies. Some were fairies made from cloth, others from glass and porcelain— all hanging in the window as if they were flying.

Hagatha found a pack of Old Maid cards that she and Clover used to play with together. From time to time, she would sit on the bed and play as if Clover were still there. Marcel caught her laughing and joking one day and his heart filled with love. It was a moment that stayed in his memory because it was so reminiscent of Hagatha when she was happy and healthy. There were many occasions when Marcel was in the house watching her with the picture cards when she was unaware he was there. Marcel noticed that she wasn't observing the rules of the game, and wondered whether Hagatha remembered them or was incapable of understanding that rules existed at all.

At that moment, curiously—incredibly—Marcel felt what he thought was his daughter's presence, and rather than comforting him he retreated from it, scared. He recognized himself in Hagatha when she gazed at a certain area of the room and asked, "Clover, is that you?" and then shook as if from fright, as though someone had answered her. It was uncanny that both Marcel and Hagatha experienced the same sensation of Clover being close to them. It had to be true. At various times, he felt a connection to his wife that was not emotional, but psychic. He was afraid that his thinking might be delusional as well, but when their eyes locked in a long stare, Marcel knew that he had experienced his daughter's presence.

Hagatha was in the habit of taking Clover's clothes from the closet and ironing them, then placing them back in the closet, each hanger the precise distance from the next, at exactly the same time every day. Though the clothes were already pressed, it didn't matter to Hagatha—she pressed them anyway. She decorated some of the hangers with Clover's ribbons as a surprise for her when she returned, and sewed ribbons on her lacy pillow cases, giving them an even more feminine appearance. The touches she added to Clover's room strengthened Marcel's belief that she was essentially herself, a woman only in need of time to recover. She filled an empty toy chest with the clothes Clover had designed and sewn from pieces of old lace and vintage wraps, and with antique buttons and bows. Every day she laid out clothes for her daughter to wear and each night she put them away, setting out Clover's pajamas ever so carefully and turning down the bed for her daughter—then climbing in herself. Hagatha even took the old sewing machine from the corner of the room and stitched together all the pieces of material Clover had saved, making the most amazing sheets and pillowcases.

The neighbors told Marcel that the shades in Clover's room were raised at the same time every morning. Hagatha would wave out the window at no one in particular, and pull down the shade at three in the afternoon, until the following day when she would perform the same ritual. She did this Mondays through Fridays only, and kept the shades raised all day on Saturday and Sunday. Marcel guessed that she was waving goodbye to Clover as she left for school and on the weekends let in the sun for her. Marcel desperately held on to his love for Hagatha. He wanted the woman he knew and loved back. His hope was constant and his patience, endless.

Though farfetched because of Hagatha's age, Marcel dreamed of having another child with his wife one day, a new brother or sister for Clover when she came back. If Clover never returned home, would Hagatha have the fortitude to give birth to and take care of a child? Would she ever be able to express the love he was certain still existed inside her? Marcel questioned his own ability to raise another child. Perhaps they could adopt. He wondered if he could withstand the fear of something unimaginable happening again. Just the thought of it was terrifying and unbearable.

Every day, despite their behavior toward her, Hagatha would leave her empty house early so that she could watch over the children at school. The name "Haggy" didn't insult her—it was the nickname her grandmother had given her when she was a child, and it was the name they had originally decided to use for the barn store. Once in a great while her mom would call her Haggy, and Marcel picked it up from her and would use it from time to time. It was "Baggy" she detested. She didn't view herself as a bag lady and was, in fact, oblivious to any change in herself at all. When Marcel would beg her to put on clean clothes, she would tell him she already had—that's what she believed.

Evelyn thought that Hagatha was on walks to get fresh air or to search for Clover in the neighborhood. It never occurred to Evelyn that she was going to the school where she once taught. Since Clover went missing, she never mentioned anything about what had happened to Hagatha afterward, to her friends or at parent-teacher meetings and activities at the school, out of loyalty to the Baggards. Evelyn wanted to protect her from being the subject of malicious rumors.

Loralee was at the University of Rhode Island and wasn't aware of Hagatha's routine of loitering around the elementary school collecting trash and picking up stray things from the school grounds. Since Evelyn believed that Hagatha was taking short walks around the neighborhood, she advised Marcel not to try following her around because she might feel trapped. That could send her back inside the house again forever. Hagatha left her house so often and for so long that Evelyn rarely came over to the house to visit.

Loralee made postcards that she sent to Hagatha, always including Clover's name in what she wrote.

Hagatha kept them in an old box that she had saved for years, and would sometimes take several of them in Clover's backpack to read on her way to school while she was walking.

When she arrived at the elementary school, the bullies would hide behind large trees, startling her as she passed by, screaming "Hey, Haggy Baggy, you stinky Haggy!" Startled, Hagatha would drop her basket of bottles and trash to the ground each time they would shout taunts at her. "Haggy Baggy, Haggy Baggy, smelly, dirty, Haggy Baggy . . . " they shouted as she walked along the perimeter of the schoolyard collecting trash.

The staff at the Robert Lewis School tried reasoning with Hagatha about wandering on the school grounds before the children went inside for class, however, they could not come to any understanding because of her stubbornness. She walked right past them, muttering and grunting under her breath for them to go away and not bother her. She refused to speak to them face to face, and after the first couple of years they stopped trying. All they felt for the bag lady was pity. Other teachers and parents were harsh, telling her that years had passed and it was time to move on.

Hagatha paid no attention, refusing to listen. After all, it was not their child who was missing, she said to herself. Some adults would use the Haggy Baggy epithet they heard from their children to refer to Hagatha because her appearance repelled them. The majority of the townspeople ostracized her; they circulated a petition to bar her from entering school grounds. Some people who had sympathized with her at the beginning turned against her, thinking her appearance somehow denigrated their community. Her sense of herself had, in part, become that of a bag lady and she had accepted the name they and the children gave her, but Hagatha still took "Baggy" derogatorily because in her mind it was insulting to her precious daughter.

"Why can't they leave me alone?" she thought. "I'm not hurting anyone." She was still Clover's mother, not a stranger on the street without a home. She recalled years ago when Clover named the store Haggy B's, and how the name fit perfectly. Now mean-spirited townspeople had taken part of the name Haggy B's to insult her. She wondered how they knew her name in the first place—someone must have told them, but to tell the truth, she didn't care.

Hagatha looked for signs of Clover every day; staying home for all those years did nothing to help find her. She saved the juice bottles and soda cans of drinks Clover used to like. The front porch of the Baggard house was lined with pails of trinkets she collected while combing the ground on her route from home to school and back. She hoarded everything and never threw anything away. Marcel watched his wife behaving nonsensically and asked himself why she couldn't free herself from the grip of her sorrow. He was impatient for the day to come when she no longer acted as if Clover had just gone missing.

When Marcel visited he straightened the lines of containers for her to make them look more presentable, but because of the multitude of things he decided to cull many items late at night, when she wasn't looking, to give the front porch a more respectable appearance for their friends and neighbors. He was aware that the neighbors weren't pleased with the appearance of his house; he had heard the rumors. But Hagatha was content with the world she had created. Just as certain people would have preferred not noticing Hagatha, she didn't notice anyone surrounding her either. She could walk by people she knew without lifting her eyes to acknowledge them. She focused beyond them as if they weren't there, just as her true self was invisible to them.

Lately, several of the neighbors approached Marcel asking him if Hagatha shouldn't be placed in a rest home or hospital for round-the-clock care—they had seen her picking at the trash barrels—but Marcel wouldn't hear of it. "Leave my wife alone! She looks in there thinking some clue may point her in the direction of our daughter. Can't you understand?" he told them. "We understand," one man replied. "But it's long past the time to find any clue that is viable." Then, to make matters worse, they complained about the mounds of debris on the front porch. "Yes, I'm doing the best I can," Marcel replied. "I take small amounts off the porch whenever I can." He would become irate and defensive, barking back, "What if it was your husband or wife, your child?" As much as they were trying to help by offering advice, they stepped away from Marcel when he reacted so furiously, knowing quite well he was right. None of them knew what it was like to grieve for a lost child. It had never happened to them. Their lives went on as usual.

The children at school continued throwing trash and dirt at Hagatha, ducking behind bushes so as not to be seen. The poor woman was just as faded as the barn store that had fallen into disrepair, no longer shiny inside or outside, covered with more cobwebs and dust year after year . . .

And during those years, the holidays came and went without much celebration. Clover used to love going to Boston to see the ice sculptures on the Common and in front of the Copley Plaza Hotel. Marcel tried his best to persuade Hagatha to go to First Night with him, but she wasn't motivated to go out; although, quite early this year she began setting out some pieces of Clover's collection of Christmas figurines to display on the ledge above the fireplace. She hadn't done that for years: placing Santa in his sleigh with the twelve reindeer prancing. Marcel took Hagatha's decorating as an encouraging sign, a breakthrough of sorts. The Christmas albums had been taken out and set on the coffee table—another promising sign.

He put flowers on the table along with a letter for Hagatha, as he did every Christmas. After the holiday was over, he disposed of the dead flowers, and he slipped the unopened letters into the desk drawer for Hagatha to read in the future, when she had healed. He wavered between leaving the letters out on the table and tucking them away, maybe tossing them out altogether. After Hagatha had opened a few of them, Marcel saw her interest and decided to save them.

Marcel spent longer and longer periods on the road away from his wife. He had to travel overseas to negotiate deals with foreign companies. During the past few years he wrote down all his emotions and observations in a journal, beginning at the time Clover went missing, to give Hagatha as a gift one day. He thought she should know how much he loved her and missed her and Clover. "We have to rekindle our love for one another," he would say to her in his letters time and time again. When he sat down next to her on the sofa he'd beg, "Please give me a chance." Again, there wasn't much of a response, just a shake of the head and then she would stand and walk aimlessly around the house.

Marcel could see that Hagatha was wandering through life as if she were alone. She took out all of Clover's Christmas treasures, Halloween costumes, Valentine's Day mementos, and odds and ends from the chest in her room—displaying them on her bed and bureau, everywhere in her room, whether it was a holiday or not. One night Marcel found her sitting in the chair beside the bed, without any expression on her face, singing Silent Night. He thought she had been making progress during the spring, but now he felt that he may have been mistaken. Her thoughts and words seemed even more jumbled. Marcel could only conclude that Hagatha was completely unaware of the changing seasons and sang whatever song randomly popped into her mind at any given moment.

CHAPTER 8

THE CHILDREN FIND OUT

Summer was approaching once again and the children were already looking forward to their vacation. (Had Clover's life stayed on course as she had planned, she would have been finished with her classes at Rhode Island School of Design for the summer, and perhaps might be doing an internship in Paris or working at Haggy B's with her mother.) The days were hot and all the kids were wearing either sundresses or shorts with tee shirts. They fanned themselves with papers or books, anything they could find. Despite the heat, Hagatha put on her coat as always and left her home closed up tight, with unopened windows and the shades pulled down so that no light could come through. The old house was so well insulated that it kept her home much cooler than it was outside. She took her usual route, avoiding the busy main street and walking on back roads and paths, weaving in and out of backyards and arriving at school as the sun beat down so brightly that her eyes were burning. She blinked and squinted until tears rolled down her face. She thrust her hand into her bag, fishing for a Kleenex to wipe her blurry eyes. Instead, she pulled out one of Clover's old tee shirts, which she held to her cheek and kissed. The kids watched her and were especially spiteful, worse than ever because of the high temperature. They yelled out to her, "You're back, you dirty bag! Ugly Haggy! Smelly Baggy, you stink! Haggy Baggy puddin' n' pie, comes to school and makes us cry!" It was the same group of bullies each time. Haggy Baggy did smell badly. Neither Evelyn nor Marcel had been close enough to Hagatha lately to notice the odor. It was the coat she wore for years now—never having it cleaned. Its sour smell came from all the food stains on it and was particularly noticeable in the damp air. Usually, she wasn't able to sense her own smell, but today was different—she could almost taste the rancid odor of her body and she gagged. Her feelings were wounded and she walked away, her eyes fixed on the ground. Suddenly, a strange feeling washed over her; her eyes began to fill with tears, but, stubbornly, she held them back. Ever since she lost her daughter she was able to tolerate anything, but not today—the heat was extreme and she was highly sensitive.

Her frail, slender body was succumbing to her emotions, breaking her down. The bullies persisted, insulting Hagatha with more names as they hurled dirt at her—handfuls of it. Some of it hit her face and entered her mouth, and she spit out the muddy paste. Some dirt entered her burnt eyes and she rubbed them, making matters worse—it was nearly impossible for her to see through her swollen eyelids.

Where were the teachers and aides? They're not watching the children as closely as they should be, Hagatha thought. Otherwise they would have intervened by now, as they usually did. She was threatened by the bullies' callous onslaught and felt violated by them. When she didn't yell back at them this time, they only intensified their name-calling, spewing out words that were nastier than the ones before, even mustering their brashness enough to call her a bitch. Suddenly a tomato struck the nape of her neck. She could feel the cool liquid of the vegetable slowly dripping down her back. An apple shot through the air, hitting her on the knee that had never quite healed and was tender most of the time. "Ouch!" she cried out as she bent down to touch the place that was sore.

Hagatha knew that this was not going to be a good day for her from the start. Her coat, which had never bothered her before, felt cumbersome. Her arms itched and she scratched them as if she'd been bitten by swarms of insects or had poison ivy. The sun had irritated her scalp and she could feel the root of each strand of hair connected to her head. She walked about jaggedly, and for the first time in many years she saw the school and children in a different light. She was tired and experienced a gnawing hunger. She raised her eyes, which were still teary from the dirt, and actually saw the faces of the beautiful children whose innocence belied their outward behavior.

Hagatha's brief happiness changed abruptly—to sadness and shame in a moment's time, as if she were naked in front of an audience. She decided to go back home, and quickly. The teasing continued as she strode past the pathway heading toward the front entrance of the school grounds followed by a gathering of children. A boy ran ahead and blocked her way. She was lost for a moment, not knowing what to do. She didn't have the strength to protest. She wanted to push him away, but she sensed there was something different about this boy. He said, "I know who you are . . . I'm not going to call you names or hurt you." She tried passing by him, but he was insistent. "I know who you are, please stop!" he implored. Although she was nervous, Hagatha paused. Something had shifted. She'd suffered enough of the children's badgering and she could not tolerate being a target or stand being called Haggy Baggy one more time. Thinking of herself as a bag lady was finally tearing her apart. She saw herself through the eyes of the children. And then the boy said softly, "I won't call you Haggy Baggy, I promise."

His voice sounded like sweet music to her ears. She moved slowly past the child, who reminded her of a student in her old class. Her heart was touched by the boy and happy memories flashed across her mind even though she hurried on her way, anxious to hide away in her house where she saw no one and nobody could see her. When he tried to follow and talk to her, she walked away even faster. Hagatha was amazed by the boy—their paths had crossed at the exact moment she was thinking about how she could no longer tolerate the bullying she was subject to for another moment. She questioned the reason he would be nice enough not to call her names and had told her as much. "Where does he come from?" she thought. "Was he one of the teacher's sons? I can't think who he looks like and I wouldn't know him anyway." She scurried away without turning back to ask the boy any questions. He yelled at her to stop, but then realized she was frightened. The other children said mean things to him, but he ignored them just as his mom and dad had told him to do.

During lunch break that day, the boy couldn't wait to tell the kids in the playground what his parents had explained to him and his twin sister about Haggy Baggy. "It's true," he said. "Her real name is Hagatha. Hagatha Baggard." The children stood quietly to listen. Timothy inhaled slowly and continued, telling them about what had happened to the lady, Haggy. The children were all ears as if he were a teacher giving them important instructions. Most of the children were in awe of her dramatic past and asked what kind of teacher she was. The bullies couldn't have cared less. The one bully who had started calling Hagatha "Haggy Baggy" was aware of her true name; the other bullies were not.

They said that Timothy was a liar, which started to annoy the other kids. The children asked Timothy and his sister questions, and he told them all he knew about her teaching fifth grade at their elementary school and her daughter, who went missing the day before her sixteenth birthday.

"Where's her daughter now?" they asked. The kids formed a circle around Timothy and his sister Megan, speaking over each other with so many questions that Timothy couldn't respond fast enough. "I've told you all I know," Timothy said, "I don't know what happened to her daughter. No one knows—that's what my mom said. That's why Haggy wanders around the school. You can ask your parents if they know anything about her." They spoke among themselves and decided that they were going to find out what they could from their moms and dads when they went home.

One small girl was so saddened by what Timothy said that she began to cry. "Maybe we can do something to help her. We can look for her little girl after school." Timothy tried to console her, explaining that she had gone missing a long time ago, and that she wouldn't be a young girl anymore. "Oh . . . but we can still look, can't we?" Timothy didn't have an answer for her; he just shook his head and smiled. The few bullies who were unmoved by Timothy's speech accused him of making up the whole story to get attention, saying that if he felt so sorry for the old bag lady he should go live with her.

"Yeah, sure, she lost her kid," one boy said

sarcastically. "I bet she doesn't have any kids, and if she does that doesn't mean she can come to our school and stink it up. We don't want her here." All the children, excluding the handful of bullies, talked about Haggy Baggy on their way home from school. The next day they gathered in the playground to discuss what Haggy Baggy had been trying to teach them for years about staying safe on the street.

The kids decided to walk together with the younger children who lived closest to them so they would never have to walk alone, especially now since they were scared. They spoke to the children in other grades at sports meets and other after-school activities, telling them Hagatha's story and advising them not to pay attention to the bullies and to stay away from them. The children understood that Hagatha's child went missing and was never found. The teachers heard the stories the children repeated and were proud of them for taking control of the situation by walking the younger children. They really had been listening to Hagatha all along.

There was a renewed awareness of Clover's case in the town. The group of bullies continued badgering the children, calling the boys "bag lady lovers," and the girls "nasty Haggys." They didn't pay attention and weren't affected by them— Timothy saw to that. Clover was fresh in their minds and they defended Hagatha against the bullies' taunts.

News traveled from school to school. Timothy acted in a manner that was beyond his years, and led the other children in calling the safety precautions "Haggy's Way." It was a unanimous decision. Although it had been years since Clover had gone missing, the children behaved as if her disappearance had just occurred. They didn't know that Haggy had a husband or that she lived in a beautiful house in town.

Hagatha's story was alive in the imaginations of the children and their parents, who now responded as urgently as the day Clover disappeared. It was Haggy's Way for the children to stay in pairs until their parents came to pick them up. The children took the lead. Timothy and his classmates understood that Haggy had been telling them to take precautions all this time. The older kids agreed to take down the license plate number of any stranger following them in a car, and to go to the nearest house or building. They formed small groups of kid "private eyes" who watched for anything strange going on. The teachers were astounded by the maturity they showed. All the kids finally listened to what the bag lady, Haggy Baggy, had been telling them for years about the safety rules. One of the middle school boys was so excited he told everyone his idea about publishing a newsletter to keep the whole school up to date about safety issues.

CHAPTER 9

RENEWAL AND RESPECT

The week that followed the schoolyard incident was trying for Hagatha. That day, she went home after the incident with the tomato and meeting Timothy and sat down on the floor behind the back door in her kitchen with her coat on and her basket and bag beside her. Tomato stuck to the back of her neck, mixing with her salty sweat. She didn't move for several days; she stayed right there, without having anything to eat and sipping from the water bottle she kept in Clover's backpack. Her tongue was dry and her stomach was empty, yet she remained sitting there on the floor, immobilized, and sleeping intermittently after shedding many tears. This drained every bit of energy from her body, but her will was strong.

When she finally stood up she was faint and braced herself against the kitchen table. Once she was stable, she drank water from the kitchen faucet, filling her stomach until it felt full. Hagatha walked around the rooms of her home. It seemed as if she were viewing her house through a different lens—everything looked new to her. Returning to the kitchen, she turned on the faucet in the sink again and ran the water until it was as cold as it could be. She was so thirsty she leaned over and drank without bothering to use a glass, gulping down mouthfuls of cold water in between breaths until her belly cramped. She splashed her face with cool water. She felt refreshed.

Instead of staying in Clover's room all day as she usually did, she sat on the living room floor with stacks of photo albums she had collected. She looked at each page and every single photograph in the photo albums, slowly and carefully, sometimes speaking aloud to the photos as she laughed and cried. The open box of candies Marcel had left was on the living room coffee table and Hagatha absentmindedly popped one in her mouth. The taste exploded. She shut her eyes and savored the dark chocolate melting on her tongue. When she opened her eyes, she fixed her attention on old snapshots of her mother and herself. She spoke out loud, saying "Oh Mom, look at us!" and re-experienced their bond, which was exceptionally close, as if they were connected by some inexplicable force.

She had pushed away both parents and all her relatives during her ordeal, but it was letting go of her relationship with her own mother that disturbed her most. Crying, she blurted out, "I'm so sorry, Mom. I've hurt you and Dad. Please forgive me!"

She hadn't realized what she'd done until now. Her mother was the one person who understood her better than anyone else, and was there to support her, whatever the circumstances. "Why didn't I see?" she asked out loud. She had punished herself and her mother by shutting her mother out of her life, as she did to everyone. She questioned why she had done that over and over. "I needed you, Mom, in the same way Clover needs me. I see that now."

The tears dripped down her cheeks like the water from the faucet that she had left running. Hagatha recalled sharing moments of relaxation watching TV with her mother and laughing at the silly commercials so hard that they cried. She and Clover often used to do the same. Memories of cutting the tops off of strawberries and preparing Sunday dinners crowded her mind. She remembered that she loved her mom's garlic mashed potatoes, fried onions, and chicken with fresh carrots from the vegetable garden—and oh, those fresh strawberries slathered with homemade whipped cream on top of yellow pound cake. She recalled her mother-in-law's cakes with French cream frosting, and how Clover would scrape the sides of any bowl of frosting with two fingers and greedily lick the frosting off. Hagatha's stomach roared as she thought about what she wanted to eat. Various foods went flashing through her head, but what she wished most for was turkey with stuffing and sweet potatoes topped with melted butter and walnuts! Her hunger gnawed at her empty stomach.

She pictured her mother helping with Clover when she was a baby and felt warmth toward her that she hadn't experienced in years. She gripped the old photograph, uttering, "Mom, oh Mom, what have I done? I didn't mean to shut you out. I was lost; I want you to come back. I've alienated you and I am so sorry." Hagatha cried and cried. Huge tears of sorrow rolled down her cheeks, leaving trails of clean skin in the dirt on her face, then continuing their path down and falling from her cheeks onto her soiled clothing, dropping smudges of dirt on the photographs that were on her lap. "Oh no!" she cried out, and dabbed at the grimy drops of water.

Finally, without a second thought, she removed her heavy coat and went to the kitchen to make hot chocolate and toast. Hagatha ignored the trembling of her hands and the way her knees buckled ever so slightly. She needed food. She recalled how Clover used to drink her hot chocolate with heaps of Marshmallow Fluff floating on the top, melting into the liquid. The taste of chocolate and the texture of the bread were exquisite. She had to eat slowly. "Mmm," she murmured. Each bite was incredible. She opened the cabinets, frantically looking for marshmallows though there were none to be found, and said out loud, "I must remember to buy them." Still hungry, she opened boxes of cookies, swallowing them one after another until her shrunken stomach cramped and was stretched as far as her body would allow.

She glanced over to the wall where her artwork

hung. Then she stared at her stained, worn coat on the floor and pushed it aside. The children were right—it did smell. Hagatha felt differently than before, and saw things as they were, not tinged by her grief. Suddenly, a wave of emotion overcame her. There were beads of perspiration on her forehead and upper lip. With a renewed sense of life, she rushed upstairs, lifting the shades in Clover's room to let in the sunlight. She was signaling to Clover that her mother was here for her. Opening shade after shade, she let the glowing sunshine into all of the rooms. Hagatha felt alive!

The photographs remained downstairs on the living room floor, scattered about in piles. She walked around her house inspecting everything, even her grandmother's ivory-colored china figurines set way behind the glass of her wooden cabinets. She and Clover had hand-painted them to make them come alive. Together, they named each piece inside the cabinet. She smiled at the wonderful memories her house evoked.

She envisioned Clover, her hair long and silky with blonde streaks interspersed throughout the layers of chestnut brown, the color of her hair since she was a child of three or four. She saw Clover sitting on her small rocking chair next to the couch, but only for a split second. It was a mirage that vanished as quickly as it came.

Hagatha remembered the awful day she was raging with anger and destroyed so many of her collectible glass pieces, smashing them on the hardwood and porch floors—blown glass vases and candlesticks, hand-carved glasses, and china bowls—the things she loved the most and were irreplaceable, like Clover.

Her head felt like it was bursting as she sensed herself awakening to the reality of her surroundings. She could feel heat radiating throughout her body in rushes. Hagatha slowly walked to the bathroom. "I have to take a cool shower," she said, "I'm so hot." The heat had gotten to her. Leaving her underwear on, she stepped into the cold water and felt relieved; she washed the worn-out items while she was wearing them, the sudsy water sliding down her legs and covering her in thick lather. She rubbed her skin with the fragrant soap, smelling the freshness she adored. The dryness of her skin was pronounced and she would need the special creams that Marcel lovingly massaged into her skin when he would come home from work after he showered her. The jars of lemon cold cream were lined up on the shelf above the sink, some half-full and others brand new and ready to be used.

She wanted to wash her hair and clean her clothing to look like herself again, but when she started washing her long, tangled hair a thought passed through her mind about Clover's silken hair and how she loved to comb it. She stopped abruptly, her hair only half-done and dripping froth from the shampoo. Hagatha stood in the shower allowing the water to rinse off what remained of the soap and shampoo. She picked up the residue from the tomato on the floor of the shower, stepped out onto the tiles and grabbed her old bathrobe that still hung from a brass hook on the back of the bathroom door. Her hair would dry on its own. Even without rinsing all the soap entirely away, she felt new and looked vibrant.

Although she stayed within the boundaries of her comfort zone, as restrictive as it was, Hagatha experienced a spark of her old energy. She threw her dirty clothes in the sink to wash. She resolved to take her usual route tomorrow whether or not the children teased her because, she believed, she was taking abuse from the children for Clover's sake. Descending the stairs, she had a change of heart, deciding she would prefer staying in the living room for the rest of the day sitting amid her photographs, happily reliving cherished moments of her past. She washed out her old clothes with her renewed strength and hung them over the shower doors. She had to wait until they dried—her clothes were like a second skin and she felt stripped when she wasn't wearing them. Hagatha put on Clover's pajamas, a worn pair she wore all the time that were soft to the touch, and as time passed she fell asleep dreaming about Clover when she was three years old.

It was nearly impossible for Hagatha to veer from the routine she repeated every day, but when she left her house the next day dressed in her slightly damp clothes she did something she hadn't done for years—she peeked over to the darkened barn that once held so much promise. She observed the flowers blooming in the yard and the paint of the barn, faded from its original vibrant color. She thought about her husband and felt the loss of his love and the loneliness of living without him. Her distorted way of thinking then resurfaced and propelled her forward, walking in the direction of the school with her bag and basket. Hagatha was a few minutes late and expected to miss the children, but when she walked up the sidewalk to the front gates all the children were gathered together as if they had been waiting for her, Haggy Baggy! They had been waiting a full week for her to return. Hagatha didn't know what to think. Frightened, she stepped back and wanted to turn and run from all the children, who were together in a large crowd. She didn't feel as though she could tolerate the many insults that would be tossed in her direction like all the other times. Now that she was confronting them she felt stripped and vulnerable because she had thrown her coat aside in the living room and had forgotten to wear its protective layer when she went out. At the same time she was relieved that she hadn't put on the coat—the heaviness she usually felt was gone, and her clothes felt lighter as they dried in the warmth of the sun.

She wrapped her arms around her body to protect herself. She was confused. "Why are they staring at me?" she thought. "Perhaps I look different without my coat, or they're expecting me to speak to them." She was terrified. Her glance darted up and down and around her, as if she feared someone was about to take her away. Holding her basket close, she wanted desperately to speak to the children but she was unable to form the words.

This morning wasn't like the other mornings, when the children shouted out her nickname. They politely said, "Good morning, Miss Haggy." One of the bullies who had thrown tomatoes at her lowered the tone of his voice and said, "Hello, Miss Haggy." The other tough kids stayed on the sidelines making faces. Some other boys who had thrown small rocks at her sheepishly waved, walking away ashamed like dogs with their tails between their legs. She looked at their expressions. She could see by their faces that they were humble and showed more respect for her than before. Each of the other children approached her, one by one, genuinely wishing her a good morning. She was stunned by the children's behavior and was speechless. She could only nod when a little girl handed her the card she had made with white construction paper and a rainbow of colored crayons.

For an instant she felt as if she were a teacher again—a teacher without a voice. There were a couple of girls whose hair and clothing reminded her of the picture of Clover she kept in her mind. The boy Timothy and his twin sister Megan timidly handed Hagatha a brown paper bag. "We brought you lunch," he said. "We made it ourselves." Inside was a tuna salad sandwich along with an apple and some large homemade chocolate chip cookies. They smiled as they offered her the food and she extended her shaky hand, aware for the first time that her nails were ragged and her hands were still dirty looking. She accepted their gift saying softly, "For me?" "Yes!" Timothy answered as the bell was ringing one last time. The children were late and they hurried into their classrooms. Timothy and Megan stood together as they said, "See you after school, Miss Haggy!"

Hagatha, whose arms were still wrapped around her torso, let them relax down by her sides, although she held on tightly to the construction paper card, her lunch bag, and basket. She didn't feel as if she had to protect herself once the children went inside. A cool breeze flowed past her and goose bumps prickled her sensitive skin. She sensed her body during that moment and felt inexplicably alive. Her clarity of mind was returning. She searched the ground for a comfortable place to rest in the sunlight.

As she sat on the grass, Hagatha noticed how silken and green it was. She ran her fingers back and forth across the blades of grass thinking how she hadn't appreciated nature for such a long time and how beautiful it was. Her mind wandered. She thought back to memories of family celebrations held outside on the green grass and wildflower patches next to the barn. She thought of the red, white, and blue colors of the Fourth of July and Labor Day barbecues with friends and family and the feasts she prepared for those gatherings. Leaning back on her arms, she dreamed of Christmas dinners and the vases of red roses spread throughout the house, and how Clover would select a few roses to leave a trail of petals leading from the foyer to the magnificent tree.

Clover always decorated the tables in the blistering heat of the Fourth of July and put red, white, and blue sprinkles on the cupcakes; she enjoyed baking and made sure everyone had a taste of her cupcakes. When she was younger, Hagatha and Marcel always took Clover to the Esplanade on the Fourth of July to listen to the Boston Pops and watch the fireworks afterward sitting on a blanket next to the Charles River. As larger crowds gathered on the Charles over the years, Marcel changed his mind about going to the Hatch Shell, opting to stay home and watch the fireworks on local TV or from their patio, often with guests who came as much for the barbecued burgers as they did for the clear view.

Along with those many other memories, Hagatha remembered the day she and Marcel sat on the grass picking clover, the day when they decided the name of their child. She felt the gentle morning breeze against her rough, weathered cheeks and Marcel came to mind. "Oh, how much I miss him," she mused, and the weight of her heart lifted. She ate her lunch as if she had never tasted food before and when she finished she still wanted more. "Tuna," she said aloud. "Oh, how I've missed eating tuna sandwiches," she lamented, and for a moment she thought about Marcel because he loved her recipe for tuna salad and raved about her sandwiches. She wondered if Timothy was aware of her fondness for tuna fish sandwiches or whether it was just a coincidence that he had made her one for lunch.

Her loneliness had evaporated, at least for the moment. She was looking forward to seeing the children after school, how great it would be to see their smiling faces without their usual abuse. But then, suddenly, her mood shifted and she felt differently, frightened of reality and compelled to leave at that very moment to go home. It was as if a dark cloud had passed overhead, obstructing the sun from shining on her. The children wouldn't see her that day when they left school or any other day soon. Hagatha understood that it was time for her to stop wandering the school grounds and go home for good. She wasn't aware that she had finally gotten her message about safety across to the children or that she would be missed; she assumed they were feeling sorry for her. Hagatha didn't realize just how much the children were looking forward to seeing her. The cobwebs that obscured her perception had to be removed like cleaning the cobwebs from the old, abandoned barn—carefully.

CHAPTER 10

BIG SURPRISE

There would be more turmoil; nothing could stay as it was. Haggy Baggy, the lonely soul who had been wandering for so long, was overcome by the kindness the children had shown her that morning at school. It touched her heart, but left her feeling puzzled and confused. She would feel awkward going back to the school now. Hagatha went directly home and stayed inside with all the shades pulled down so tightly there wasn't even a dusting of sunlight. She didn't resume her habit of opening Clover's shade to wave goodbye in the morning. Unlike the front door that required a different key to open, the kitchen door, which she usually left unlocked, was now not only locked but deadbolted to keep everyone out. In her paranoia she lost sight of the fact that even Clover wouldn't be able to get in by that door with her key, not just friends like Evelyn. Hagatha was desperate and felt an urgent need to be completely alone. Her certainty about

Clover returning was suddenly gone. She realized it had been years since the day Clover went missing. It was as if she were standing at the shoreline and a huge wave caught her from behind and washed over her. She was overcome by reality and needed solitude; time to herself to regain her strength and see her life clearly once again, a life without her daughter.

She shook her head up and down, talking to herself as she roamed the house. Hagatha began by searching in the attic, opening every trunk and box of her grandmother's belongings, family albums from the past, even toys she'd played with as a child. She felt like she was a blank slate, learning about herself from the very beginning. She tossed things everywhere. It appeared as though she was verging on either a breakthrough or a complete breakdown. Marcel left messages for Hagatha on the machine. She would run to the phone to hear the sound of his voice, and for the first time she listened intently to his proclamations of love for her.

When her groceries were delivered, the delivery boy had to leave her order outside on the small back porch rather than simply walking into the kitchen to drop things off. This concerned the boy. He found a note Hagatha left him asking for Marshmallow Fluff and bags of miniature marshmallows. In the note, she asked the boy to invite Loralee to her house for hot chocolate—he thought her request was rather odd, and after his third attempt to get inside he assumed that there must be some kind of problem.

On his next run, he put three bags of marshmallows at the back door along with a large jar of the Fluff. Worried, he spoke to the manager of the small store who suggested that he tell Evelyn instead of Loralee.

The boy was so concerned that he decided to walk up the street to their house to tell them about Hagatha. Evelyn was aware of her new habit of locking the doors, and she could tell that the delivery boy was upset because he couldn't get in. She thought it was time to tell Marcel. It had been slightly under three weeks since Hagatha began to stay indoors, never unlocking the doors for anyone or opening the windows. She did crack the door open to slip through and quickly pick up the marshmallows for her hot chocolate and the rest of her order, which consisted of cans of tuna and a jar of mayonnaise. After thinking long and hard, Loralee and her mom decided to deal with the problem themselves rather than call Marcel, who was experiencing his own difficulties communicating with Hagatha. Not only was she unresponsive, but he had been out of the country on business for a while and she was angry and distant. She neglected clearing the messages on the answering machine and eventually there wasn't any space left for him to leave word for her.

Evelyn understood that Hagatha was using the cocoa and marshmallows to reach out to Loralee. Loralee couldn't make sense of Hagatha's message about the hot chocolate until her mother explained it. Evelyn and a few other neighbors spoke to the boy, and they attempted to get inside the house, but because Hagatha had deadbolted the door Evelyn's key didn't work.

Evelyn and two other neighbors left home-cooked meals at the door to entice their cloistered friend. Occasionally, Hagatha took the trays into the house and would leave an empty tray on the doorstep. They were encouraged by her putting out the trays and tried to get her to come to the door several times. The answer was always the same: "I'm resting now. I'm fine. Please go."

"Are you eating enough?" they would ask. "Do you have enough food?" She would reply, "Yes, thank you. Please go away!" And then there would be silence.

When Hagatha liked the food—and when she didn't—there wasn't a crumb left on the plate. She was eating only small portions of the foods she did like and was tossing the rest out the window for the birds to scavenge. Although Marcel would put seed in the bird feeders whenever he visited, the blue jays, robins, and sparrows preferred the daily fare she spread about, as did the squirrels that always got their share. Evelyn and the other neighbors assumed that Hagatha was eating what they brought to the house; however, she was simply leaving the empty trays outside whether she had eaten the food or not.

Evelyn and Loralee once dug through the trash for evidence of food to make sure Hagatha was eating, but found nothing except for empty cans of tuna, used cocoa packets, and plastic bags from the marshmallows. They already knew that Hagatha was drinking cocoa and marshmallows because she had asked for them every time she placed an order. Loralee knew the kinds of foods that she liked and it was easy to please her—Evelyn brought her sweet things to eat, particularly chocolates from the bakery Hagatha loved so much. The door of her house still remained locked. Evelyn and Loralee cooked sweet potatoes with butter and brown sugar for Hagatha, who wrote notes thanking them for being such good friends to Clover. Loralee cherished those pieces of paper as much as her mother's wedding pearls. Evelyn never became discouraged; she made her homemade apple and peach pies that she knew Hagatha loved. Hagatha would pick the fruit out of the pie and give the crusts to the birds.

Summer vacation was ending and Hagatha had stayed indoors for the long, hot summer. She often passed the time reading and re-reading the cherished card the little girl from school had made for her. Inside, in scrawled black crayon, it said, "Please, can you be my teacher? Love, Allyson." She was so moved by the innocence of the child's question that it spurred her to recall the person she used to be. Evelyn would write notes to her suggesting that she come over to visit, but she still wasn't ready to leave her seclusion. Hagatha wrote back saying that she wanted to be alone and would she please understand. To placate her, Evelyn stayed away, but she continued writing to her, taping the notes to the back door where Hagatha was likely to find them.

When school re-opened, the children noticed that Haggy wasn't there. They made a pact to search for her in the mornings and afternoons, every moment when they were not in school. No one knew Hagatha's address just yet. The children wondered why she vanished—they'd been civil and friendly toward her. One boy said that when grown-ups go away it's because they die.

"No, no," one little girl said, "Sometimes they die, but sometimes they go to Florida."

"That's right," another child said. "My grandma goes away to Florida every winter and she doesn't die; she always comes back!"

Two of the kindergarten teachers who were monitoring the playground overheard the children's conversation.

"Kids say the silliest things!" one of the teachers commented.

"They sure do," the other said, trying her best not to break out in laughter.

Haggy Baggy had become part of their daily routine over the years and her absence in September was felt by both children and adults alike. Throughout their vacation time, a few of the teachers who were friendly outside of class and knew her neighbors discussed Hagatha. The remaining teachers she'd worked with when she taught were especially concerned, and had written letters to her without receiving any response. Then again, there were those who didn't expect a letter anyway because of the condition they understood she was in, but that didn't stop the flow of letters from them. Marcel once noticed the pile of letters on Clover's vanity wrapped and tied with ribbon. A few of the teachers even made attempts to visit her at home, but to no avail. She stood perfectly still listening to their knocks and the chiming of the doorbell. She always froze, unable to move forward. She was familiar with most of them, and though she never answered, she felt grateful they came nonetheless.

When Evelyn and Loralee finally spoke with Marcel, they described Hagatha's erratic eating habits and told him about her self-imposed isolation. Although they told him that she spoke more when they stood outside the front door, Marcel, who was working abroad, was beside himself with worry about her state of mind and returned home immediately.

He was desperate. "This can't continue anymore," he informed his boss. Marcel's boss arranged for someone to temporarily fill his position—he valued Marcel more than any other person who worked for his company. "Don't worry," his boss told him. "Do what you have to do. It's family." Although Marcel was mentally and physically exhausted, he went right from the airport to his office to drop off some important files, and then went straight home. Entering the house through the front door, he saw Clover's treasures from the attic placed in rows in all the hallways. He went in and put his suitcases down next to the living room couch. The family albums were strewn about everywhere.

Hagatha didn't speak to her husband. She just stared at Marcel, smiled, and continued pacing around the house. Marcel had called ahead to the grocery store to tell them he was at home and to bring a few additional items. "The back door will be unlocked," he informed them.

He turned the lock and slid open the deadbolt on the back door so that the boy could deliver the groceries, and taped a list of items on the door for him to bring the next day. Marcel quietly moved around the house trying not to disturb Hagatha. He sensed that something about her was different. Since he was unable to walk easily through the clutter, Marcel picked up some of the things, putting them away while leaving the rest so Hagatha wouldn't have a temper fit. As she watched him, it was apparent that she didn't mind his attempts to get the house in order—that certainly was a change in behavior from what he had become used to.

Although they looked for her each day, the children at school still did not see their Haggy Baggy. They asked the teachers to help them search. Some suspected that she had gone away forever because of them, while others believed beyond a doubt that she had died.

Timothy explained the children's worry and guilt to several teachers he found in the teachers' lounge, telling them what the children were thinking, including the younger children's fears that she had gone to Florida and might never return. They told Timothy they went by Mrs. Baggard's home but she wouldn't open the door. They told him they had spoken with a close neighbor who told them that Mrs. Baggard was staying inside her home and refused to speak to anyone. "She's very much alive," one teacher was quick to note. "There's no reason for any of you to worry."

"Do you think I could go to see her?" Timothy asked.

He wasn't surprised when they replied, "No Tim, that's out of the question. We shouldn't bother her. It's her choice to be alone." The teachers explained that Mrs. Baggard didn't leave on the children's account, but for a number of reasons unrelated to them. "That's all we know," they said.

"Yeah, I kinda' knew you'd say no," Timothy replied.

Timothy left, saddened. He thought, "What if Mrs. Baggard were my mother? How would I help her?" Timothy had a good heart, and his teachers were certain that one day he would be involved in some kind of service to others. The teachers discussed Hagatha's disappearance after Timothy had gone, guessing that she hadn't been to school because of the children learning about her identity, or that perhaps the children's warm greeting had upset her in some way. They were positive that bouncing back and forth to her house wouldn't work, nor would their letters. Their hands were tied. All they could do was wait until someone came up with a solution that would bring her out of her shell.

The teachers became more focused on Hagatha.

They would look out their windows for her as they taught their classes. Every day, the children were anxious. They fidgeted in their seats and couldn't wait for recess to search for their Haggy. Some of them still brought extra food to give her in case she reappeared. They held their breath each day until the last bell rang, but Haggy didn't appear then either. They placed their gifts—bags of food labeled "Haggy"—on the steps in case she came. They always found the bags on the steps the next morning. The teachers told them not to waste food anymore, and to be patient for Haggy to appear. When they were in class, the children would crane their necks to see if she was outside the classroom window. The teachers couldn't help but notice the disappointment on their faces and that their concentration was not as it should be. The more artistic children doodled during class, drawing likenesses of Haggy in the margins of their notebooks.

All the teachers asked their classes to write a story about Haggy Baggy, their schoolyard friend, and the children were excited about their new assignment. Timothy let his teacher know that they had stopped calling her Haggy Baggy, preferring Haggy instead; but, he said, he supposed it was all right to call her Haggy Baggy so long as it wasn't meant to insult her. "Something more has to be done," the principal told the teachers during a brief meeting they held after school about Hagatha. "The children's concern for her welfare is overwhelming."

During class, one of the younger children raised her hand and explained that Haggy probably had the flu because her own mom kept her home for a week when she was sick. "Well then, you could write your story about that," her teacher told her. The children made fun of her and the teachers couldn't help but laugh out loud just as they did when one of the children said that Haggy must have gone to Florida to retire from her job of collecting cans and bottles.

Outside the classrooms, in the hallways the teachers whispered to one another about how cute the little girl was when she spoke about Haggy's mother keeping her at home because she had the flu. The other kids kept on criticizing the little girl, saying that Haggy was far too old for her mother to stay with her when she was sick, but the girl stuck to her story, not understanding what the other children meant. "I don't believe you. Haggy has a mom. Everyone does . . . " and with that she sat back down and pouted.

Days passed, and then weeks. The school's principal visited all the classrooms, attempting to motivate the students to get back to their work, telling them that Haggy would be disappointed in them if their grades continued to fall because she couldn't be at school. That seemed to work; Hagatha was an inspiration to the children and they buckled down. Both the teachers and students were back on track.

The principal worried that something serious might have happened to Hagatha Baggard. She hadn't responded to anyone in quite some time. He wanted answers and would do whatever was necessary to find out about Mrs. Baggard, even if that meant contacting her husband. The stories the children had written were piled high to give to Mr. Baggard for his wife. The principal decided to meet with the staff and students in the auditorium to discuss what they could do jointly to coax Hagatha out of her house. Several meetings were held by the principal and faculty, even the parents who knew her attended. Although only a handful of parents, who called Hagatha by her nickname Haggy, were critical of her appearance and odor, the majority were eager to do whatever they could despite the way she looked and the oddness of her behavior. One woman, a parent, stood up and defended her in an emotional speech, saying that she could relate to Hagatha and that if her own daughter went missing she would lose it too. The principal stressed that her appearance was the least of his concerns about her and that appearance wasn't an issue. "Mrs. Baggard is a wonderful woman inside, and beauty, as we all know, is only skin deep." He commented that there should be meetings about how the children dressed instead, and that was truly an issue to be discussed in all the schools. Questions were asked and ideas brought up, and considerable headway was made toward updating the school's safety policies as well, particularly making the students aware of paying attention to their surroundings rather than walking and texting at the same time.

Two more weeks passed and still there was no sign of her. Their worries grew. When Principal Walker spoke with Evelyn, she explained that Hagatha was the same as far as she knew and that her husband, who now had been inside the house, might be able to provide more details. They were relieved and shared the information with the children.

Loralee called Marcel on his cell phone.

He answered with, "Hello! Marcel speaking!"

Loralee replied, "Loralee speaking!" and both laughed. She explained, "Hi Mr. Baggard. My mom asked me to call you. She went to a meeting about Mrs. B. at the school. Apparently, the school, the parents, and the children all wanted to know how she was doing."

Marcel assured Loralee, "Hagatha isn't visibly ill at all, but there has been a change in her that I can't quite pinpoint just yet."

Loralee said, "It seems that the whole school would like to do something special for her, to help her in some way. They've had several meetings."

"I'm a bit confused, though. I didn't know that the principal even knew about my wife."

"Is it okay if my mom gives the principal your cell phone number? He wants to speak to you about Mrs. B."

"Loralee, you tell your mom that it's fine to share my cell phone number with the school principal or anyone on the staff." Marcel responded positively, but, like Loralee, wasn't certain how the principal knew so much about Hagatha.

Evelyn had gone to the meetings at school and received a note from the principal's secretary. Evelyn gave the secretary Mr. Baggard's cell phone number to discuss what they could do to help Hagatha. She knew that after all these years Marcel would be receptive to any idea if it would bring his wife back to her normal self.

When all the children and teachers had contributed their final ideas, they put a plan together that was certain to surprise Haggy. Of course, they needed Mr. Baggard's consent. The principal called him, and after describing the relationship his wife recently shared with the children of the school, Marcel was even more surprised than Loralee. "I never would've guessed that," he said. "I never knew she was there every day. Now I understand where she went and that she had another purpose when she was walking. Evelyn will be happy to know about this too," he told Principal Walker. "We've told Evelyn already," the principal replied. Loralee decided to join the group at the school, and—since she was Clover's best friend—became one of the lead volunteers on the committee. Marcel was extremely grateful that Evelyn and Loralee had gotten involved.

His heart was warmed by the children's interest in his wife's wellbeing. He requested that Principal Walker drop formalities and call him Marcel, and assured him that he would be there to help in any way possible now that he was at home. Marcel was so happy he told everyone in his family and close friends that he would bring a gift for Hagatha, one that was long overdue—a highly unexpected surprise.

When a couple of the teachers asked about the gift, he wouldn't tell them anything more than that it would have special meaning for his wife and Clover. They wondered what it could possibly be, but were not forward enough to ask him again. The happiness that came through Marcel's voice when he spoke about his gift added to their curiosity. Marcel was intent on keeping the gift a secret, except perhaps for telling one other person. He was so eager to get started he gazed up at the sky and asked Clover for her approval. He believed the glittering of the stars and his memory of the sound of her voice was her reply to him. He recalled that when Clover used to watch the night sky, she would ask the stars for guidance and the glittering of those stars was their response to her. The excitement Marcel felt changed his demeanor. On the phone he told his parents that he felt as if he were going on a first date with Hagatha, and their hearts were overjoyed for him.

All the schools were involved in making the surprise, as was everyone else in town. Just as the young bullies were ignored by the other children, the adults who didn't approve of Hagatha were also disregarded. Marcel, Evelyn, and Loralee were so proud of what everyone was accomplishing for Hagatha. Marcel introduced himself to the children at the elementary, middle, and high school. The teachers told Marcel about two of the boys who had made Hagatha into a target—he spoke to each of the boys one-on-one, and both boys were apologetic and asked Marcel for his forgiveness. They were by far a minority among the many people who were trying to help her, and they appeared awkward and foolish in comparison to everyone else. Marcel thanked them for their cooperation, although he suspected the principal and their parents had a hand in their sudden change of heart.

Marcel wasn't angry, but he made sure to tell them, "On any given day you might find a member of your own family or a friend in the same position as my wife; perhaps even one of you. Taunting and teasing is mean-spirited and childish," Marcel added, "and is totally unacceptable at any age. To endure the loss of a child is a fate I don't wish on any family."

The boys sensed the depth of Marcel's sorrow and his message was clear to them. "We're really sorry, Sir," said one of the boys. "We didn't believe the story about what happened to Hag . . . I mean Mrs. Baggard, and she looked like a homeless lady. Now we understand that every person deserves respect even if they look different or dirty. It was wrong to judge her. Neither of us will make fun of a homeless person ever again."

"That's right, boys. No one ever knows why people do what they do." Judging Hagatha without having insight into her sadness created prejudice against her, and Marcel was overcome with happiness that the majority of people finally recognized the depths of her prolonged grief.

Thanksgiving was coming and Christmas would follow quickly enough. In the Baggard household, this usually meant another lonely holiday.

"Not this year," Marcel vowed. "I won't stand for it!" He paused to remember how the three of them would go shopping together for a large tree, always at least six feet tall. He smiled as he recalled how Clover loved eating Thanksgiving dinner with the family. She especially savored her mother's stuffing, which she ate in her own way, putting heaps of it in a bowl and dipping each spoonful in mashed potatoes and then the gravy. Whenever Hagatha was making the stuffing, Clover would tell her, "More raisins and chestnuts, please."

"Mmm, delicious," she would say. "When I'm married I'm going to make stuffing just like yours and give the leftovers to my dog." "Yes, I'm sure you will," her mother would reply.

Clover's job was to make the cranberry sauce with Grandma Maura. More than cooking, Clover looked forward to Grandma's hugs and kisses while they made the sauce. They enjoyed the best of times together, listening to the big band music Grandma loved, and Grandma telling stories from when she was a young girl. While they were cooking, they'd dance around the kitchen.

The week of, and after, the holiday, Marcel would make Clover turkey sandwiches with mayonnaise for lunch at school, thick ones with stuffing and cranberry sauce, a smear of mashed potatoes, and a couple of shakes of black pepper. It was traditional for Hagatha to buy two turkeys, one for the guests, and one for themselves that would last beyond the holiday for leftovers. The apple and pumpkin pies Marcel's brother made were usually finished within a few days.

Like the rest of Marcel's family, his brother Edward lived in France, but further south near the Mediterranean. He didn't have a phone, and the only way to reach him was by corresponding through letters that were delivered by courier. When Clover first went missing, Edward flew to see his brother as soon as he received the news she had disappeared. Staying at the home of one of Marcel's old friends, he went out with his brother, taking a leave from his work and searching for over four months. He was as heartbroken as Marcel. His promise to his niece that she could come to France after she finished high school and they would tour the countryside meant little now and tugged at his heartstrings. He and Clover maintained their closeness by exchanging postcards over the years. Clover made sure to affix a sticker to every card she sent; it was her signature. Edward believed that Clover would come back someday. He had to continue to believe that in order to cope.

Marcel let the principal know that Christmas was Clover's favorite holiday. She would always want to start decorating right after Halloween each year, which, her mother told her, was far too early, but

Clover insisted.

In his imagination, Marcel saw his eight-year-old daughter dressed in the chipmunk costume Hagatha had sewn, made from brown, furry material, with a hood and ears. Then there was the time Hagatha had painted a red nose with black whiskers on Clover's face and Clover told her mom she wanted to look like a dog, not a cat.

"C'mon Mom, I love dogs," Clover said.

"I know you do, except cats' eyes are exquisite. I'll practice, and next year you can be a dog," she promised. Clover was not enthused. She said, "Well, I may look like a cat, but I'll bark like a dog!" Picturing their daughter dressed as a cat and barking like a dog sent Hagatha and Marcel into peals of laughter that made their bellies cramp.

Clover would lecture them about how eating turkey followed Halloween. Then shopping for Christmas presents came the next day after Thanksgiving dinner. "You can find the best things the earlier you shop," she pointed out. "Why wait so long? Shopping for Christmas after Halloween is even better!"

"But you know Mom, it's true," she would say. "If you wait too long to buy presents all the special things are gone and then you'll end up buying whatever's left." Clover would then put her hands on her hips and in an adult-like tone explain to her mother that because the weather was colder after Halloween, shopping for presents was an appropriate thing to do rather than waiting. This always brought a smile to Hagatha's face as well as a laugh.

Even from a young age Clover simply loved to shop. Her love of shopping in small, eclectic stores wasn't centered on herself, but on the joy she felt buying gifts for others. This was a generosity she learned from her mother and father, as well as both her grandmothers, who devoted their time and money to causes that held meaning for them.

Clover used to pick wildflowers from the garden in spring and summer, tie them in bunches with old cloth ribbons, and sell them for five dollars each. Marcel's mother taught Clover how to give the wrappings a French flair by using ribbons and lace doilies. In addition to her allowance, she had money to spend as she wished. Each present she gave was wrapped in decorative paper that she designed herself, using the brown bags she collected when the holiday was near. Sometimes she would use newspaper for wrapping, topping off the boxes with bouquets of ribbon. She recycled everything, including empty food cartons.

Every year she went to stores, door by door, going inside to ask for broken items she could recycle. She went to tobacco shops asking them for empty cigar boxes, which she'd air out, sew lavender scented linings into, then use for containers for cookies or as jewelry boxes with broken gems glued on them. She made her friends cigar box handbags with braided, straw handles.

"Oh yes, Clover's a talented young girl," Marcel's

dad would say. "She's going places, you wait and see!" Now, Marcel flinched as he recalled those words.

Clover and her mom made cookies for the firemen and policemen. They appreciated the boxes as much as the cookies. She would bring gifts she made to the center for unwed mothers and watch as smiles lit up their faces. Just before Christmas Eve, Clover and Marcel would help out in a kitchen at the homeless shelter for men, ladling portions of food onto the plates of the men waiting in line. Marcel recalled the happiness Clover generated with her smile and high spirits as they worked, conversing with the men and making the wait in line seem shorter. Sometimes she would sit at the long tables telling them stories she learned from the books she read in English class or heard from her grandmother. They adored her.

When she was younger, Clover would ask her dad, "Could a couple of them come home with us to eat?"

"But then all the other men would have to come," her dad answered. "It's not fair that only a few visit."

"Yes, Dad. I suppose you're right," she would reply.

There were so many other memorable moments that brought a smile to Marcel's face. He tried to follow his mother's advice when she said, "Remember the happy times and Clover's smile; your sorrow will be lighter to bear."

CHAPTER 11

SCHOOL AND HOME PROJECTS

The Robert Lewis Elementary and Middle School was filled with the joy of the early holiday spirit because of the surprise they were planning with Mr. Baggard for their Haggy. Joy spread beyond the school to the parents of students and to other people in the community.

Timothy and Megan wanted to help in any way they could, even asking for more projects to take on. Megan suggested that she and Timothy bake a cake, or at least decorate it, but their mom and dad proposed something else they might do, something much better with more meaning—something that would last.

"Help us with an idea," Megan said.

"Can you and the other children make lots of angels to hang from the barn ceiling?" their mother asked. "Mr. Baggard told me that Clover loved fairies and angels and was fascinated by pigs with wings."

"Yes, yes, we'll all make the angels," Timothy and Megan replied at the same time. "Good idea, Mom." Megan nudged her brother, saying, "We don't know anything about baking or decorating cakes anyway, do we?"

"I sure don't," Timothy replied with a self-conscious laugh. "Maybe we could've gotten help if we asked the Life Skills cooking teacher. Now we'll need help from the art teacher to make flying pigs. Too bad there's no more cake. I was looking forward to testing the batter and the frosting."

Megan put her finger to her lip. "Me too," she said. "It's too bad we won't be a making cake, especially because I could've made another cake for us!"

"Yeah, you're a glutton for sweets," Timothy added as his sister waved her hand in the air to him. "See ya," he said as he took off through the door.

They were so excited to make angels and flying pigs instead of cake that they couldn't wait to go to school the next morning to tell the other children. The atmosphere in the classroom was electric as they all worked every day after school in the art room until there were boxfuls of angels. Each angel was original, and one more unique than the next. Fairies were made with pastel-colored paper with shimmering stars the art teacher ordered especially for the project. The few pigs the children made were pink and had angelic expressions. An artistic fifth-grader, Noah, made an enormous angel using large sheets of white construction paper—the biggest of all the angels and flying creatures by far. Timothy and Megan made an angel for Haggy's desk with her name on it.

Even Loralee got involved helping the fifth and sixth graders. Knowing Clover as well as she did, she thought that making fairies and angels was a great idea. She made a mobile using a larger angel with two fairies and a pig, and mounted an enlarged photograph of Clover on white cardboard with fairy stickers glued around the border for Hagatha's desk in the barn.

Marcel was wowed by her work, and Loralee felt proud of what she had made, as were her parents. "So there is some artist in you," Marcel observed. The boys from the high school who took woodworking class refinished several pieces of the old barn furniture and made a wooden frame for Loralee's picture of Clover. Marcel, who snuck into the classroom at night, painted some of the older pieces the boys had sanded in modern, bright colors. The chairs and tables were impressive, brought to life again by everyone's efforts. The art teachers took photos for a page in the school newspaper under the heading "School Projects."

Marcel couldn't wait for Hagatha to see what they'd done. He pictured her delight when she walked into the barn. With each passing day Hagatha spoke more—a "yes" here and a "thank you" there. These were positive signs, but she still needed her space.

Marcel prayed daily that Hagatha would allow

people to approach her. She still hadn't spoken in full sentences since he'd been staying at the house, and he presumed that his being there was responsible for her relative silence. So Marcel busied himself with errands outside the house and asked Evelyn to watch Hagatha in his place; she seemed to be less tense when she was alone with Evelyn and Loralee. "It must be a girl thing," he quipped. Evelyn had to agree. "Why yes, I believe it is," she replied, and they both laughed.

Marcel spoke to his parents and told his father that he was exuberant in anticipation of the surprise. His mother, who was listening on another extension, expressed as much excitement as her son, though she tempered it with advice. "Don't push her too hard," she told Marcel. "Be sure to prepare Hagatha for her surprise; tell her about it in tidbits." "I can't prepare her, it just has to happen—good or bad" Marcel replied. "It's a surprise, after all."

Marcel's parents were coming to the States for the barn celebration, and were planning to place pictures of Clover when she was just a toddler visiting Paris around the house when they came to town, along with photographs Hagatha had sent them of past Christmases with Clover as a child opening her presents early in the morning. It would be a celebration of Clover as much as it was a celebration of the holiday.

Marcel told his parents that the handmade topper angel for the tree that was in the attic would be taken out of its box this year for the first time since Clover went missing. "A symbol of hope and Clover's presence," he said. And then, without any warning, Marcel was suddenly overwhelmed by a crushing wave of sorrow.

His parents didn't know what to do as they listened to his loud, bellowing wails. "The holidays are a difficult time," his mother said. "Let it all out. Both of you have endured so many painful years, it's okay." After several minutes, he pulled himself together. He told his mom and dad that Christmas was supposed to be a happy holiday, yet at the same time he was sorrowful because of Clover. "Christmas will never be the same without her," he said. He told them how much he loved them and appreciated the letters and flowers they sent Hagatha year after year. No more words were needed, just his expression of love and gratitude. "I love you both. See you soon," he said. "Yes, my dear one. We're looking forward to seeing both of you," his mother said.

Marcel decided that the anniversary of Clover's birthday would be the perfect day for him to give Hagatha his surprise gift. Afterward, on Christmas Day, they would celebrate the grand opening of Haggy B's. Everyone, both friends and family, were anxious and in suspense. This time Marcel was resolved never to close the store again, and never to allow wasted time to pass between himself and Hagatha. "I'll employ someone if I have to until she comes around," Marcel declared.

"Marcel, why don't you stay with us?" Evelyn

asked. "We have an empty room just waiting for you. There's no need to go back to the rooming house . . . " "Yes, thank you, Evelyn," Marcel replied, obviously relieved and grateful. Loralee was staying with her parents until the New Year and helped Marcel maneuver with his suitcases up the stairway to his room. Loralee told her mother that she knew what Mr. Baggard's secret surprise was, and her mother encouraged her to keep it to herself.

Evelyn said, "Even though I really want to know, I can wait. That way, it'll remain a surprise." They had invited Marcel to stay for as long as he wished without any worry. Robert would be temporarily dislodged from his man cave in the attic, but he didn't mind, he spent a lot of time out of the house doing volunteer work. A true friend, he had already done his share of work renovating the barn in every spare moment he had.

Marcel's bedroom was a large loft in the attic where Robert's collection of clocks was displayed. It was charming and private, and it was possible for him to see a partial view of his house. He looked out the window trying to catch a glimpse of the kitchen windows, but all he could see were scores of trees totally blocking his view of them. Yet that was enough for him—just the proximity to Hagatha and his home was comforting. Every so often Robert yelled up to Marcel, checking to see if he was okay. "I'm doing very well, thanks," he'd call down. "Great room—the view is spectacular!" The room's surround sound system was equally as good and at night Marcel enjoyed listening to the "Pops" type music he found searching through Robert's cd's, calming piano and violin renditions of popular songs he was familiar with from listening to the car radio.

The similarities between Loralee and Clover that Marcel noticed in Loralee's mannerisms soothed rather than upset him. Her clothes and her way of dressing reminded him of Clover's signature style, unique and somewhat quirky.

Marcel hadn't paid much attention to the room before on the few occasions he'd visited Robert; now he saw each and every detail. He examined the clocks Loralee's dad collected, and thought how unusual they were. He had never really gotten close to Robert in the same way Evelyn and Loralee were friends with Hagatha and Clover. Marcel wanted to change that, to take more time with friends rather than working so hard. The ticking of the clocks was somehow relaxing. Some of them were from other countries, and that gave Marcel the inspiration to give Robert a clock from France and Evelyn and Loralee a gift for all their help the next time he traveled outside the U.S. He already knew what he would send Evelyn and Loralee for Christmas— bouquets of dried flowers and French lace and a broach his mother had mailed to his office. He wanted them to have a keepsake and planned to give them a card signed "Hagatha and our Clover." He pictured the flowers brightening up their living room for years to come. Marcel had time to pause now that he had taken a well-deserved vacation from his job. He'd visited all the towns in the area, posting new signs about Clover and searching the stores Hagatha used to shop in for the perfect small gift to give her in addition to her surprise.

Marcel visited one of Hagatha's favorite stores, which was two towns over, where he found a flying pig and a dog with wings for Clover and a gift for Hagatha, a paperweight with clover flowers inside— quite a find, he thought. "It was meant to be," the owner said. As Marcel sat on the chair next to his bed looking at the gifts, he honed in on the tick, tick, ticking of one of the clocks. Suddenly his perception shifted. He felt a cold breeze blow through the room and brush past him as though an angel had touched him. The air encircled him, wrapping closely around his body, at first cold then warm and pleasing.

"She's still alive. I can feel her," Marcel said aloud. "Yes, I can. Please, answer my prayers and let it be that she comes home someday!" Marcel felt what his wife had been sensing for years. Across the room the window was slightly open, although the curtains were perfectly still. His thoughts turned to Clover and the realm of spirits and angels. He thought how curious his daughter was about such things. It was possible, he thought, that Clover could have visited him in her spirit form—that was not beyond his system of beliefs. He was certain it had happened. Clover was sending a message that she was all right, although it wasn't clear to him whether she was dead or alive. Perhaps she had seen the puppy, Sam— Hagatha's surprise gift—curled up sleeping in the box next to her dad's bed. She always spoke about life beyond this life and believed in cosmic energy, that if there were enough good energy, good things would happen. He imagined that all the energies were surrounding him, pulling together and passing by him.

The shiver he experienced reminded him of the many times he sat in the car picking up Clover from Loralee's house after a play date or a sleepover in the winter, when the heater in the car hadn't warmed up yet. Chilly air passed by him again as he reminisced. Marcel stood up and walked over to the window, where a tree stood outside without the slightest movement of a branch or a leaf. He could see that there were other trees swaying in the wind. "How strange," he said. He paused for a moment then closed the window, leaving it opened a crack. He envisioned his daughter's bright smile as she lifted her gaze up to meet his. Marcel's heart skipped a beat as he breathed in the cold air that passed through the window. He had a feeling Clover was there next to him and her presence, whether real or imagined, comforted him and restored his faith in her return.

"I know that you're here with me on earth every day I walk my path of life," he said, "I can feel you." He picked up Sammy and nestled with the puppy for a moment and wept. "I know you're out there somewhere; I can feel you on earth or in heaven. Where are you?" he managed to say amid the tears which continued flowing until he could no longer cry anymore. "You must be alive!" he exclaimed. "I believe your spirit is here with us!"

Marcel stood up on his feet and put Sam back into his box. He had to maintain his strength of mind for Hagatha's sake. The day had been exhausting, first from crying on the phone with his parents and now again in the guest room. He leaned over to pat Sam's head as the puppy desperately scratched the sides of his box to get out, whining, and looking up at Marcel with his soft, brown eyes. "It's okay, boy. It's okay," he said. "You'll be free of that cardboard box soon. Go to sleep now . . . " Marcel looked into Sammy's eyes and smiled.

The skies turned dark as evening finally arrived. It was a bitter cold winter's eve. The homes in the town were lit magnificently, the church bells rang, and the excitement of Christmas was in the air. The promise of the holiday filled the atmosphere with anticipation.

There was nothing festive about the Baggard home, where even the indoor lights were turned off. The outside view of the house was stark and lacked the golden glow of life taking place inside its walls. But Marcel had seen to it that the bleakness of the house wouldn't last for long; lights were strung along the bushes up the stairway and along the path to the barn and were ready to be lit once Marcel gave the signal.

Although he eagerly anticipated Hagatha's surprise, he wondered whether she could tolerate the excitement without becoming overwhelmed and running to hide in Clover's room with the door shut, cut off from everyone. The counselor at school had advised Marcel to be cautious about stressing Hagatha too much.

"Your pace should be slow, and speak softly," the counselor advised him. He agreed, and so did all the parents, who were a bit afraid of Marcel presenting her with too many gifts too soon. Marcel glanced at Sam and knew in his heart that when she saw the little guy, she would love him and her heart would open up again. "I should've thought of getting her a puppy years ago," Marcel lamented. "But she may not have been ready then."

He asked Loralee to place the other gift boxes for Hagatha under the tree at his house at a time when Hagatha wasn't paying attention or when they were walking out to the barn.

"Can you can sneak in quickly and arrange them on the floor?" Marcel requested of Loralee.

"Of course, Mr. B., no problem." Loralee responded excitedly, looking forward to helping to give Mrs. B. a happy, peaceful holiday.

CHAPTER 12

TRIBUTE TO CLOVER

There was a new plaque dedicated to the memory of Clover that hung on the wall nearest the principal's office at the Robert Lewis School. Some of Clover's artwork was there, framed by the art teacher, Mr. Russo, an old friend of Hagatha's. Marcel had a poem Clover had written long ago framed, and he hung it on the wall alongside her art. The teacher and his students decorated the hallway walls with her work, and the work of other talented children as well. The stories the children had written about Haggy were in a glass shadowbox from ceiling to floor. The writing had brought tears to the eyes of the parents and staff. Other parents of abducted children from surrounding Massachusetts cities and towns heard about the wall dedicated to missing children and hung up the art of their own children.

The wall received attention on the front page of the Emerson town newspaper, and from some newspapers in the towns nearby. *The Boston Globe* and the *Boston Herald* picked up the story and wrote articles about the tribute the children and parents had created together. The principal decided to keep the wall up as a fixture in the school to remind students and their parents of the missing children. Their celebration brought people together in the same way Clover's disappearance united them the night Clover went missing years ago.

Marcel's blog received commentary from parents of missing children, who knew all too well about the responsibility of parents to monitor children's activity on the internet and their whereabouts going to, and coming home from, school. Marcel used the blog as a means of promoting Hagatha's buddy system, Haggy's Way, for children walking without adult supervision. Several online companies wrote that they were also concerned about children's safety and that they shared a responsibility with parents to protect children from predators. One company was designing a system that would assign an identification number when a phone was purchased for any child under eighteen; the child's number would appear when he or she visited questionable sites in order to block young people from going to certain online destinations. The registered number would have to be presented before a child could enter an adult site or chat room. Marcel contacted the company and was told that this safeguard would be in place as soon as they fixed some glitches. They were working on several updates already. "Good," Marcel told the company's president, "it's long overdue."

"Yesterday wasn't soon enough," said Marcel, who was sufficiently alarmed by the increasing number of missing children every year to tell the companies to make safeguarding them on the internet a priority.

A woman from Connecticut contacted Marcel and told him about her daughter, who vanished when she was five years old and had been miraculously found when she was twelve. An online photograph of the little girl led to her disappearance. The girl's kindergarten teacher had posted a portrait of her class, and soon afterward she was taken from her backyard after she had walked home from school with two friends, one that was seven years old and the other, eleven. Her daughter was in the backyard while the sitter was in the kitchen preparing cookies and milk, and within a matter of minutes she was gone. Seven years later, a woman recognized the child from a computer image posted on the internet that had been manipulated to show a likeness of her as she became older. The woman called the police and the girl was rescued from a small town in upstate New York. "My daughter hadn't been harmed—a true blessing—but all those years away from the family were confusing for her and an unbelievable strain on all of us." The woman who kidnapped the little girl and brought her to New York said that her own child, who bore a striking resemblance to the girl, had passed away from cancer when she was five. No immediate charges were brought against her; she was admitted to a mental health facility for psychiatric evaluation.

Marcel put a recent photograph of the girl on the wall, with a hand-painted "Always Believe" plaque and a framed inspirational poem next to it. It was truly miraculous that she had been found and it gave Marcel more hope that Clover was still alive. The girl's mother said she would try to attend the special day, although her family might be going out of town for the holidays and if so would visit the barn after Christmas. The internet had caused her daughter's disappearance, but also facilitated their efforts in finding her. Marcel was so moved by the mother's experience that he called Loralee to tell her about it, and Loralee was in turn heartened by the woman's tale.

More letters arrived at the Emerson school with "Attention to the Principal" or "To the Baggard Family" written on them. Some of the letters conveyed sad stories, though there were as many optimistic letters that told of children who had been found. Searching the media archives at Emerson High, a teacher found a photograph of Clover smiling near one of her creations, a photograph that she and her family had never seen. The teacher had copies of the photograph made and sent them to Mr. Baggard as a Christmas gift. The mail basket to the side of his front door was stacked with mail he hadn't opened yet, cards from people he knew and others from concerned strangers who had gotten his home address. He knew it would take months just to open the envelopes and that he would need someone to help respond to all of them. Evelyn hadn't picked up the mail at the school for the Baggards in a few days, and she dropped the cards that had accumulated into the cardboard box that she'd been using over the years to save them for Hagatha to read one day when she was back to her old self.

Inspired by the wall at the school, Loralee had another plaque made, this one dedicated to Hagatha and her safety rules. The woodworking class at Emerson High carved "Never Walk Alone, Be Safe" as the inscription on the wooden tablet, which was hung on the wall in the center of all the artwork and photographs.

The next surprise was the utmost tribute to Clover. Some of the policemen who had searched for Clover and remembered the cigar boxes full of cookies she had given them, donated their time helping to rebuild the barn, cleaning day and night, making repairs to the windows and roof with Marcel and Robert. Even after Clover went missing, Marcel served the homeless meals on holidays, and a few of the homeless men he knew who had once been in construction offered to help with the barn as soon as they found out about the project, wanting nothing more than a warm meal in return. They promised Mr. Baggard they would go to work for Clover's sake, and vowed not to drink on the job. It was a wonderful surprise that Clover's disappearance had helped them to make a breakthrough in their own lives. The homeless men told Marcel that contributing to the project for Clover motivated them to recover from booze. Marcel put them in touch with organizations that would help them get good jobs with reputable companies.

Marcel thought, "If only Clover could know that."

The Emerson police department had raised a considerable sum of money for the charity they established in Clover's memory. This fund was for families of missing children who couldn't afford to take time off from work to search for them.

Marcel donated a substantial amount of money he and Hagatha had put aside for Clover's college fund. Marcel still kept a considerable amount for Clover, praying for a miracle that would bring her home someday, just as the twelve-year-old girl had been found. Both sets of grandparents gave large portions of their retirement savings for funding the search for Clover as well as the fund in her name, and the aunts, uncles, and cousins in Hagatha's family sent large checks. Marcel's family in France raised more than one hundred thousand francs, which they donated to several organizations for missing children in Clover's name. Donations came in as word spread about the fund.

A wealthy donor who had made his fortune from a start-up tech company, a man who'd once been one of the homeless men Clover had read to, gave three hundred and fifty thousand dollars to build a wing in the school for a small theater with a stage and a podium for speakers—all given in Clover's name. After his wife and children died in a car accident, he left his company in his partner's hands and gave up his privileged world to live a life of poverty on the streets. No one knew he was a multi-millionaire, but to Clover he had always been rich in spirit. She had lavished attention on him, reading him bestselling novels she found in the town library. Donating money in Clover's name gave his life renewed purpose. The only conditions he had donating the auditorium was that it be used for the students to read their original stories, and that he remain anonymous. He revealed himself to Marcel only.

Marcel was extremely excited that his family was traveling from France to attend the grand barn fest. All of them were happy to make the trip for this very special occasion, and to give emotional support to Marcel and Hagatha—whatever they needed. Although Hagatha had turned away family and friends, Marcel stayed in touch, grabbing a moment here and there during the workday to speak to his family. They tried giving extra money to Marcel but he refused. They had already given large portions of their savings for the search when Clover first went missing.

Hagatha's parents and grandparents missed her, and kept their faith that this time she would be willing to speak to them. Both families were always sympathetic and understanding.

David and Maura prayed that this time their daughter would not withdraw and seclude herself from her loved ones. One word from her would be enough to compensate for all the years without her. They were all too familiar with her tendency to want to be alone at times, especially as a child and adolescent, but she had taken her occasional introversion to an extreme these past years, punishing herself and all those who knew and loved her.

Maura arrived early and stayed with some dear friends. She volunteered to help out at the elementary school near the house for as long as she planned to stay, waiting with the children to be picked up so that they would be watched by another set of eyes, and working with the children in the after-school program in their arts and crafts class.

The barn was lit up inside and filled with family, neighbors, close friends, firemen and policemen, school faculty, and older children who used to be in Mrs. Baggard's class long ago.

There were a few former students who brought along photographs of Clover when she was at birthday parties at their houses, and candid photos of her in art class mugging in silly poses. There was a photo of Clover at the local animal rescue, flanked on all sides by a slew of dogs.

They hoped that this would be Hagatha's breakthrough. She didn't have any idea about what was going to happen. She never saw or heard anyone working outside her house.

This was the day her husband hoped would arrive, an opportunity to bring his wife back to life. He was overcome with profound happiness at the thought of Hagatha returning to her former self. At the same time, he recognized and was prepared for the possibility that, having so many people to confront, she might escape into herself, but he felt he had to do it; she seemed to be emotionally ready now. Hagatha's parents were also aware that their daughter might respond with fear and reject them again.

Earlier, Marcel discussed his concerns with the school counselor he contacted about Hagatha's ability to handle the stress of the occasion. She told him that she'd be there at the barn festival in case she was needed, which eased Marcel's worry about his wife's state of mind.

Evelyn expressed concern about Hagatha being caught off-guard. "This may shock her," she told him, "but maybe that's what will bring her back." Marcel promised not to pressure her with more than she could handle. The caution they expressed was certainly warranted. Evelyn planned to stay close by her side in the barn. She then spoke with three substitute teachers who'd volunteered to work in the store in Hagatha's place because she wasn't ready—and might never be ready. Marcel planned to donate the money the store made to Clover's Fund. The teachers assured Marcel that there would always be someone available to work and that the store wasn't going to close as it had before. "That's a promise!" they told him.

CHAPTER 13

THE BIG DAY COMES

Marcel glanced at his house for a moment. He walked from the sidewalk up the path to the steps the children had shoveled from the light snowfall the day before. The white lights he and the children hung decorated the bushes and were waiting to be turned on. Marcel was holding his precious gift in a box that Loralee had wrapped in plain brown paper for him. She had wrapped the cover of the box separately so Hagatha could open it easily, with breathing holes cut out of the sides and complete with ribbons decorating the top—exactly as Clover would have done it.

Marcel had confided in Loralee about the contents of the box one night when she was hinting around about what may be in it. She just couldn't keep her suspicions secret. She had heard the puppy whimpering several times, and told Marcel that was how she knew exactly what he had in store for Hagatha. She was the only one who knew what the surprise was. She gave the puppy a goodnight kiss every night after that. Still, Marcel was doing his best to keep it secret from her parents, taking care to keep the pup hidden with a ticking clock he borrowed and put in his box to comfort and quiet him.

Now the puppy was whining and scratching to get out of the box. Marcel lifted the cover and, peeking inside, said, "Hold on, Sam. We're here!" Sam looked up as if he understood and rested his head down on his paws. Marcel was so nervous his mouth was dry. He pictured Hagatha still wearing the old, worn dress, the same one she had been wearing for so many years. He almost turned back, but realized that his visit didn't have to be like all the other times he slipped into the house through the back door to watch Hagatha mope about—not this time; he would not be run out of his own home. Tonight would be different, the beginning of a new life together. "I have to put my foot down," he said to Sam, "no matter what happens."

Rather than using his key he rang the bell, something he never did. The familiar chimes sounded like the day he installed them. Sam was quiet, as if by magic he knew he would be out of the box in a few moments. The heads of the guests peered around from inside the barn doors, curious, wanting to see Hagatha if she stepped out as she opened the door to greet her husband. She clung to the door. The distance from the front door to the barn was too far for them to see her receive her gift, and oh, how they wished she would step outside when she answered Marcel's ring to see her face full of surprise.

Hagatha's voice meekly called out, "Who is it?" Marcel then knocked until she opened the door a few inches, and then a few inches more. He could see the silhouette of his wife on the wall behind her, with her narrow shoulders and her gaze directed downward. Slowly, she lifted her eyes. Tears rolled down her face like raindrops on a flower petal as she opened the door for him. He saw she was puzzled that he had been ringing the bell. She was wearing the same old clothes she had always worn since Clover's disappearance, as he suspected she would. She had become like a portrait of herself in his mind, just like a faded mural in an alleyway, washed out, the colors not as bright as they were when it was first painted. Yet, at the same time, he felt that he was seeing through Hagatha to her very soul.

"It's Clover's birthday," she said again and again, sobbing. Marcel stepped in the doorway. "Yes, it is," he said. "She will always be here with us." The barn doors closed. The family could no longer watch, but held each other's hands in suspense. Hagatha and Marcel were alone in the silence of the moment. The air was dense. The two of them felt as though they were enclosed in a cocoon.

Time was suspended as they stood there perfectly still, both recalling the face of their missing daughter. Guests in the barn whispered about the joy and sorrow they imagined Marcel and Hagatha were experiencing on their child's birthday. They could all sense the depth of the couple's emotion. Even the guests who didn't know them well were teary-eyed.

Marcel ventured a few steps closer and held Hagatha in his arms, embracing her even though the box with Sammy in it came between them. She returned his embrace. Despite her wiry hair and worn-out clothes, he smelled her usual scent and saw her beauty. He wept as he told her, "It's been so long, Hagatha. I love you and I've missed you so much. Please come back to me today; it's a special day for Clover and for you. Come back for her sake!" he begged. "Our future depends on it." He felt a connection between the two of them he hadn't felt in years. He would have dropped to his knees if he hadn't been holding the box with Sam inside. Hagatha fixed her gaze on her husband's sympathetic face while he kissed both her cheeks and then her lips. Hagatha melted. She let her guard down for the first time in a very long time. He felt the warmth of her love surging through him, calming him like their early days together. He pushed the hair away from her face and ran his fingers down her shoulder. Marcel stepped backward and Hagatha did as well. Both of them were in a state of bliss and confusion.

The moment was especially poignant for Hagatha. She had been looking at her wedding photographs, which were scattered across the living room floor, and it occurred to her that she and Marcel should speak together today—and there he was! "An angel brought him here today," Hagatha thought, "our angel Clover."

Marcel paused for a moment and, looking over Hagatha's shoulder, saw the photographs lying here and there, but in the dim lighting couldn't make out which albums she had taken out since his last short visit. He was overjoyed, and convinced they had created a connection between them—and didn't want to lose it ever again!

The box Marcel was carrying began moving and Hagatha, feeling tentative, stepped back, asking with questioning eyes what was inside. "What is it?" she asked, her voice trembling.

"It's one of your gifts. Please, open it now" Marcel pleaded with Hagatha.

"Gifts? I don't want any gifts. It's not my birthday." Marcel begged, and said, "Please Hagatha . . . I know you'll like it." He extended his arms holding the box in his hands. "Please open it."

Hagatha hesitated, and like a child said, "No, I don't want to."

"But you don't have a choice," he softly replied, "what's inside is depending on you to live."

"Oh, no, don't say that!" she protested.

"No, no. Don't be afraid, dear." Marcel spoke in an even gentler tone, trying to calm her anxieties.

She lifted the cover of the box and the ribbons fell to the side. With her shaky fingers she opened the box all the way and there, inside, was the puppy—just like the one Clover had wished for so many years before.

"This is a gift honoring our daughter's memory on her birthday," Marcel explained patiently to Hagatha.

Sam was sitting on one of Clover's old tee shirts, one that they bought her on a trip during school vacation. Hagatha covered her mouth with both hands as she gasped in surprise and her eyes welled in a sea of tears. "Marcel, it's a puppy!"

"Yes it is, and he needs you." She picked up the puppy, using Clover's shirt to blanket him against the cold, and held Sam to her chest.

"Oh, my," she whispered, "we planned to give our daughter this gift on her birthday."

"Yes, my dear, we did. Clover would want you to have it on her day," Marcel told Hagatha. She felt the puppy's collar and noticed there was a shiny silver tag attached to it. Her tears awash in her eyes, and without her reading glasses, she could still make out that it was engraved with the words "Sam— Always, Clover" and the date of Clover's birth.

"This is your new home," Marcel said to Sam as Hagatha nuzzled the affectionate puppy in her arms.

"Yes, oh my dear Clover, how I miss you." She hugged Sam. Tears of joy streamed down her face, the droplets dampening the puppy's fur. Hagatha was beside herself with happiness.

"Come," Marcel said as he placed the box on the floor, "there is one more surprise!"

"No, no," she said in a frightened tone of voice as she backed away, holding onto Sam for dear life. "No more, please!" she pleaded. "I can't bear it!"

But Marcel insisted, and said he would not accept any more no's. Hagatha had little fight left as she listened to her desperate husband. He was so pleased she was speaking, and he didn't want to lose more time.

Marcel kept his eye on Hagatha, looking for possible signs of exhaustion. Her breathing appeared to be unusually rapid and he was afraid she might faint. He wrapped his arms and coat around his wife to keep her balance and led her to the back door to go outside. He observed her and thought, "She's not light-headed, just excited—that's all." He could tell she welcomed his touch. She held onto the puppy and put him under Marcel's coat to stay warm.

One of the neighbors had turned on the white lights strung across the bushes in the front and surrounding the house, and the glow lent warmth to the scene. They ventured out down the pathway across a light dusting of snow, Marcel in his work boots and Hagatha in Clover's fuzzy high-top bedroom slippers with rubber soles.

Marcel asked her, "Please Hagatha, trust me and close your eyes tightly. Please keep them shut until I tell you to open them."

Hagatha said nothing. Her breathing was shallow and she gasped for air. She took each short footstep tentatively, stopping between steps to regain her balance and holding Sam over her heart. Marcel could tell that his wife was weak and likely undernourished.

His thoughts wandered to the many times he and

Hagatha took brisk walks in the snow, pulling Clover behind them on her sled.

He asked, "Do you remember when we pulled Clover across the yard to the next street to go sledding with Evelyn and Loralee?"

"Yes, of course I do," she replied in a calmer tone. He envisioned the aluminum saucer Hagatha bought for Clover. She had bragged about getting it brand new at a tag sale. Clover was young and it was etched in Marcel's mind, particularly the way Clover fearlessly slid down hills at the park on their afternoon outings.

Hagatha asked, "Do you remember how shiny the saucer was when I first bought it?"

"Of course I do, dear." He noticed the creaky sound his boots made on the snow and wondered if she was recalling other memories of Clover in the winter. He could almost taste the hot chocolate and marshmallows Hagatha used to make to warm them after their outdoor adventures. He had no idea she practically lived on cocoa and marshmallows lately. He'd seen the ingredients in the kitchen cabinets and wondered if she was making the cocoa for herself or stocking it for when Clover returned. They continued walking.

Marcel realized he had been silent while he was recalling memories of his family and said, "Don't worry my dear, I'm here with you."

"Please? Can I open my eyes?"

"It's just a few more feet. Don't worry, please."

Hagatha's heart was pounding; she couldn't

imagine what it was! Her heart skipped a beat as it occurred to her for a second that Clover had returned—but no, "Marcel would've told me if it was our Clover," she thought. "He would never, never keep that secret." Marcel could feel her body quivering from nervousness and the cold. Again, he reassured Hagatha. She squeezed Marcel's hand. Hagatha knew Marcel was much too sensitive to shock her that way, but at the same time, however unlikely it was, she wished that Clover was the surprise Marcel was leading her toward.

When they were in front of the barn doors Marcel said, "Trust me."

"I do," she replied.

Then he asked, " Hagatha please open your eyes now and look up!"

It took a few moments of opening and closing her eyes to be able to focus. There, on the top of the doors, was a freshly painted red and pink sign with silver trim that said "Haggy B's Barn," and carved underneath was a new sign that hung on a chain that read "Always, Sweet Memories of our Angel, Clover," with a carved angel attached to it. The wings of the angel were decorated with a border of tiny pink and blue bulbs. Hagatha's eyes were opened as widely as possible as she stared, not needing her glasses to see! When Hagatha first read the sign she laughed with happiness. As she smiled she felt an inexplicable warmth fill her soul, as if Clover's presence had entered her body and was sustaining her. It wasn't the only time Hagatha experienced that warmth rising and rushing through her chest and limbs. When she lay in Clover's bed wrapped up in the covers, she often experienced the same sensation—as if Clover were sending her a message.

The barn doors, which were ajar, opened wide. Twinkling white bulbs were strung across the ceiling. There, crowded at the entrance, stood her family and friends, and Hagatha smiled even more broadly, never averting her eyes. She was stunned by the beauty of the barn she had always cherished. Hagatha was happy, and it showed!

The school counselor took Marcel firmly by his arms and whispered, "Good job! She looks fine. Just stay beside her or have a family member or friend close by."

"Yes of course," Marcel replied. The children were lined up on both sides of the barn, making a path for Hagatha and Marcel, and as they walked Hagatha felt as though she was in a church procession making her way down the aisle to the altar. She didn't have a moment to think about how she appeared; it didn't matter.

She began to think of herself as Hagatha, not Haggy Baggy anymore. In all the excitement she caught a glimpse of the gigantic Christmas tree decorated with beautiful ornaments, glass ornaments Marcel's parents had made with pictures of Clover opening her presents on Christmas morning. How wonderful they were, Hagatha thought.

The people in the room were sedate for Hagatha's

sake, although everyone was feeling excited. There were presents from Hagatha's family underneath the tree that were wrapped in newspaper with silver and gold ribbons, the way Clover used to wrap hers. She knelt down to touch them. "Clover," she murmured, "you're here in this room. You are the angel that watches over Haggy B's." Hagatha was cradling Sam, who nuzzled against her. "And one day you'll return to us."

She gazed at the handmade angels, each one unique and flying overhead as if they had flown down and were carried on gentle air currents from heaven, and she smiled at the flying pigs suspended above her head with transparent wire from the ceiling.

Hagatha stood up and was still, mesmerized by the movement of the angelic ornaments. For a moment she was deaf to any sound in the barn. With her face lifted, she looked directly at the ceiling and experienced a sudden and marked shift in her perception, a change of mind. Thoughts poured in, and she no longer felt bereft of her daughter, but accepting of her loss. The paper angels were a consolation, reminding her that Clover must be at peace wherever she was. She perceived her body, and the sense of being alive, at that very moment in time within the space of the barn.

Then she turned her eyes away from the angels, realizing she had been the source of much hurt to those who loved her by carrying on the way she had for so many years. Suddenly, she felt the full force of regret washing over her, but at that moment Evelyn saw her pained face and came closer to hold her.

She said, "Just hold my hand. We can do it," and Hagatha's emotion subsided. For a moment, she felt serene. She looked back up, and the tentative looks she received from her aunts and uncles made her realize how lonely she had been. Regret stabbed her like a knife, yet she maintained the sense of self that had always been there, though hidden beneath the costume she wore. She knew in her heart that the last thing she wanted to do was hurt others.

Marcel watched Evelyn as she gave Hagatha the support she needed. There was a crowd around her and as Hagatha stepped further inside, everyone moved back even more. As much as her family and friends longed to hug her, they were too timid to touch her. She appeared so frail.

The counselor stayed close to Hagatha on one side, and Marcel on the other, relieving Evelyn. He was aware of his wife's altering facial expressions— he'd witnessed them many times. Marcel kissed her forehead, she squeezed his hand. A warm smile appeared across her face and her eyes sparkled.

Hagatha saw a long painted table and an antique desk chair, and sighed. Marcel was finely attuned to her moods. She might be about to break down, he thought, but she had more strength than he expected, having gained a certain amount of resilience despite, or because of, her suffering.

There was also a stuffed chair Clover had loved that needed mending. She once said that she wanted to save the old chair for when she got her dog, Sam. Marcel and Loralee both took pride in fixing it. Hagatha ran her hand over the top to feel the chair's texture, imagining that Clover was sitting on its down-filled cushion with the bright yellow and pink flower pattern. Nestled in the crook of the chair's arm was a pillow Loralee had created, with the black print of a dog's paw and yellow tassels. Marcel and Loralee were watching every move Hagatha made. Loralee took a picture to have something to remind Hagatha of this moment in her life. As Loralee looked around the room she couldn't help but notice that of all the teachers who were there, Clover's favorite teacher wasn't among them. When Loralee mentioned this to her mom, Evelyn said the teacher might have relocated to another part of the country, or that perhaps there was some other similar circumstance that prevented her from attending the barn fest. Loralee was forever loyal to Clover and kept mental track of everyone who had made an effort to help ever since her friend disappeared. It bothered her that the teacher who meant so much to Clover wasn't there. She sorely missed her best friend. She felt closer to Clover when she was near Hagatha; she shadowed her the way a parent would follow a child taking his first steps, ready to catch her if she faltered.

Hagatha placed Sam on the seat cushion, where he sat comfortably perched as if he knew the chair was his own. She recalled how Clover's slender body would sink into the cushions as she held her toy dog, reading. "Sam," she whispered, "this chair belongs to you and Clover." Hagatha pulled out the chair with the puppy on it and, picking up Sam then putting him on her lap, sat down for a second.

There was a dog bed with Sam's name on it at her feet and an old brass register on a dark, wooden table that was used many years ago by Hagatha and Clover. The children had tied a red satin ribbon around it—it looked like a package from Tiffany's. On the table was an old photograph of Clover holding the original Haggy B's sign. Photos in an antique frame sat on the table along with pictures of Loralee and Clover when they were much younger, even as early as two years old. An abundance of angels and fairies Loralee had made surrounded it.

"Yes, Clover is here!" Hagatha whispered. She stood up, and said, "My baby has come back!"

Marcel heard her comment and entertained the same thought as his wife did at that very moment, and wished Clover would come back for all to see her angelic face and smile.

The crowd of family and friends started approaching Hagatha, some standing back a few feet shedding tears of joy, some feeling more confident they could give her a hug; they were careful not to overdo the attention they gave her. Everyone spoke to her in low, soft voices when what they really wanted to do was cheer her on. They saw beyond her appearance, into her heart. Hagatha looked intently at all their faces, trying to remember who they were, amazed by their show of sentiment and enthusiasm.

She turned to her husband and, still holding Sam, thanked him in a whisper again and again, especially for waiting so long for her.

"I love you, Marcel," she said as they clasped each other's hands as if their very lives depended on it.

"I love you too," he replied. "I always have, and always will."

The fan in the center of the barn ceiling gently blew the angels and fairies as they danced a graceful ballet. Hagatha lifted her eyes to watch them. It was heavenly. This was Christmastime and it showed on everyone's face like the shimmer of the North Star. It felt like Christmas Day, but it was the spirit of Christmas that filled the barn. A hint of jazz and Christmas music could be heard playing in the background, just enough to set the mood.

Marcel moved aside to allow Hagatha's parents and grandparents to approach her. They had been waiting patiently. They kissed their daughter's forehead, holding back their joyful tears as much as possible to avoid upsetting her. When her father hugged her he tried to be strong, but broke into tears in her arms. Her mother looked on, fearing his heart couldn't take it. Hagatha collapsed into sobs and cried with such emotion that the people standing nearby began to cry too.

"I love you, my child," he said, "I don't want to lose you again. We've already lost so much. Stay, don't go away anymore." Hagatha held her father.

"Yes, Daddy, I'm here. I promise I won't go." She

continued to cry on his shoulder like a child. "Oh, Daddy, I love you so much! I'm so sorry it took me such a long time. I'm not even sure of the time that has gone by, Daddy. It seems like yesterday."

"It's all right, my child. At least you're here with us now."

When her grandma kissed Hagatha's cheek, she said, "That's my baby."

Hagatha held on tightly to her special Nan. "I love you, Nan, so very much."

Then her grandpa patted her back. "That's my special girl. And where's my other special girl?" She paused for a few moments, unaware of the Alzheimer's that plagued her grandfather. Then realizing that it was likely the family hadn't told Grandpa about Clover at all, Hagatha delicately replied, "She is here, Grandpa. Here in spirit."

Hagatha hugged Marcel's parents and said, "Mom and Dad Baggard, I love you so much!" as she expressed her love for them with many kisses.

Heartfelt emotions filled the room while the angels floated above their heads. Tears fell from Hagatha's eyes, rolling down her face as she silently cried for joy to be with her loved ones again. Her dad kept his arm around her shoulder, giving and receiving every bit of affection he could until her mom stepped in to hold her daughter again.

Hagatha sensed for months that a change was taking place deep within her heart and now, finally, she understood there were many reasons in her life to be happy again.

She thought, "This moment is one I will always remember."

She hugged her mother and father, embracing them the same way a small child would, needy of their love. She held on to them tightly. Not only did she have her memories to cherish, she had her future to look forward to—each day holding surprises, each day sharing with the ones she loved and who loved her. Loralee was taking snapshot after snapshot on her digital camera. Marcel put his arms around his parents and thanked them. He touched Loralee's shoulder lightly to get her attention. When she turned to face Marcel, he looked into her eyes and told her how much he appreciated everything she and her mom had done to make the day possible. "I know, Mr. B. There's no need to thank us. We'd do anything for Clover."

Hagatha believed with all her heart that miracles sometimes happen. She could only hope for the day when her wish for Clover's return would come true. The family knew Hagatha had returned to them and that was a blessing. The excitement had worn on her, yet she toughed it out. There were more surprises at the house for her.

During the time she was in the barn reuniting with her family, Evelyn, Robert, and Loralee slipped away to clean and set up for the celebration in Hagatha's house. Loralee arranged the presents under the tree. She and her mom placed bouquets of pink clover and vases of red roses on the hutches and bureaus. By the time Hagatha had spoken to almost all of the guests in the barn, hours had flown by. Marcel announced that he was taking her home. Walking back from the barn to the house with Marcel, Hagatha noticed the warm yellow glow emanating from the windows—all the lights and lamps were on, a sign that life was taking place inside. Amazement was written on her face as she stepped over the threshold of the front door; she could hardly believe her home was so beautifully transformed for the holidays. She made note of Marcel's brown leather duffle bag full of clothes that Robert had taken from his house and left on the first step of the stairway.

Hagatha and Marcel's mothers and Evelyn offered to help Hagatha change her clothes and wash her hair. They couldn't expect Marcel to help them—he had enough to do. Loralee anticipated helping all the women to change Hagatha's appearance so it shined as brightly as her inner glow. Hagatha's mom bathed her and fixed her knotted hair after cutting off a few inches, a project that kept them busy for quite some time. At their feet was Sam, playing and nipping at their toes. Hagatha gazed down at the playful pup with pleasure. Loralee offered to go through her closet to see what clothing might fit her slimmer body and would be fashionable. Hagatha agreed to the suggestions her mom and Loralee made; she truly appreciated their willingness to help. She knew she could never adjust to such extreme changes alone, and asked them to be patient with her and to go slowly. They could see she was anxious and a bit shaky and they stepped back to give her more space. Hagatha's mother and Marcel's mother, along with aunts and Loralee, went through her closet, getting rid of her outdated clothes and keeping those that still had tags attached. They found a bright red sweater and a new pair of white sweatpants for Hagatha to wear. Hagatha looked radiant! While they worked in the bedroom, Hagatha went downstairs and was looking at photos in the living room. The old coat, it was decided, would go to Goodwill after it was dry-cleaned—a piece of clothing she reluctantly agreed to give away.

Hagatha persuaded Marcel to stay close as she underwent each new change, and he was delighted to give her whatever she asked, saying, "My dear, I'll be by your side, I promise not to leave you." They sat alone together on the sofa. Hagatha smiled, giving a tiny laugh. She expressed her ardent wish to keep Clover's room exactly as it was at the time she went missing. It would be a sanctuary meant to keep her alive in their minds and hearts forever. Marcel agreed with her without question or debate. Sam whimpered for attention as they turned each page of the photo album that rested on Hagatha's lap.

"For always and forever," he said, "but don't take your old clothes out of the Goodwill pile to keep, promise me." "Just the one coat," she replied. "Remember, Clover gave it to me as a gift." "Yes, I do." They spoke about Clover without becoming overly emotional, trying to express their sorrow in a measured way. Her absence was just below the surface, finally not in the front of their minds, obstructing their living in the present.

CHAPTER 14

CHRISTMAS

Hagatha felt a sudden urge to go to the barn, alone. She'd been sitting too long looking at the photographs, and asked Marcel if he would please understand. "Of course, go my dear," he said. "I'm fine," she added. "I don't need anyone to go with me."

She walked out the door and went to the barn. She was awed that it was just as she imagined it so many years ago—even better than she envisioned it. Hagatha realized that many people had put their love into the barn for Clover and her, and she felt a responsibility to maintain herself for their sake as well as her own.

"I can't disappoint them," she said to Sam as she cuddled him in her arms. "I can't disappoint my daughter. I have to move on. Clover would want that. I have to be strong." Sam whimpered. "I have to believe in what I'm doing. I've missed having family for years. We'll share our lives, feeling close again, all of us remembering the good times with Clover. Right, Sammy?" She said, "Sam, do you understand?" and Sam made a high-pitched yelp in reply. She laughed. Hagatha gazed at the ceiling as she entertained thoughts of Clover when she was little, in the barn playing with her fairies and dolls. She walked about the barn, soaking in its charm until thoughts of her husband waiting for her sent her back to the house.

That night, Hagatha and Marcel sat together discussing Clover until the sun came up. She fell asleep in Marcel's arms, her head resting against his chest, and looking closely at her face, he noticed that the glow of her complexion had returned and her cheeks were rosy. He thought she appeared to be content. The weight of her grief had been lifted during the gathering and the short time she slept. She had re-entered her own life. As Hagatha lay sleeping, Maura brought them a warm blanket and served Marcel a mug of cocoa with marshmallows.

The next day, after a few hours of sleep next to Hagatha, Marcel got up and placed an advertisement in Emerson's newspaper for someone to help out in the store once it was officially open. He knew it would be weeks or longer before Hagatha finished cleaning herself up and began working, even with ample help. She needed to keep busy or she might lapse back into depression. The pace at which life was changing was demanding for Hagatha, and Christmas was fast approaching. It would have been impossible to manage without both sets of parents and Robert, Evelyn, and Loralee's help. Some of the family lived close enough to help at a moment's notice.

One night, just before Christmas Eve, after Hagatha went to sleep, Evelyn, Robert, and Marcel decorated the tree in the living room, adding Clover's vintage ornaments as a surprise for Hagatha in the morning. When Hagatha woke up and padded downstairs following the aroma of coffee and toast, she was astonished by the magnificent glow of pink lights enveloping the tree with its vintage ornaments and she instantly thought of Clover's smile. She sat on the floor with Sam, amid piles of gifts, to look at the beauty of the tree and to experience her daughter's presence in the room with her. The rest of the family made biscuits with jam in the kitchen, enjoying the morning sun beaming through the window as they waited for Hagatha and Marcel to join them.

****

Timothy and Megan answered the ad to help out in the store. They had overheard Marcel telling a teacher about the job, ran to buy up as many newspapers as they could find, and answered the ad immediately to beat out any competition. They placed the call to Marcel, who thought the twins were absolutely the right ones for Haggy B's. Timothy and Megan's mom and dad fully approved of their taking the positions because they were old enough to spend a few hours each afternoon and on weekends to give Hagatha a well-needed hand.

They would be earning enough to have some spending money, and also, in return for their working, Hagatha offered to help them with their homework. "I might be a bit rusty," she admitted, "but I can still teach."

Marcel told her it would be like riding a bike. "You can do it, honey. I know you can. It'll come back to you," he said, and Hagatha felt more confident, buoyed up by his kind words.

Loralee was so pleased that Timothy and Megan would be the ones helping out in the store; she had babysat for them when they were much younger. She knew Clover would have thought they were, without a doubt, the best choice. Loralee was also amazed when she found out that it was Timothy who had started the campaign against bullying Hagatha.

Maybe it was a coincidence, or perhaps it was fate, that the twins' birthday fell on December fifteenth, the same day as Clover's birthday. Hagatha and Marcel wished them a happy birthday, and Hagatha said that when she was feeling better, she would take them out for ice cream and a day of shopping, specifically vintage shopping if they were interested. They were thoroughly excited by the idea. Timothy collected comics and small metal soldiers in different battle poses. Being so close in age to Clover when she disappeared, the twins could at least partially fill the void she left.

Marcel figured out the hours they would work and

Hagatha approved. He assigned Loralee the task of painting a sign for the door. He taught Timothy and Megan all the important details they needed to know: paperwork, the alarm code, keys and locks, and even the hiding place for extra cash taken out of the drawer—whatever he could remember to tell them. The twins impressed Marcel with how quickly they learned. Marcel made them keys with special tags that read "H.B.'s Timothy" and "H.B.'s Megan." Timothy showed Hagatha the keys for the store. "Here is your set of keys to open Haggy B's Barn," Timothy told her with a big smile. "Mr. B. gave them to me." The key ring was made with charms of Clover's flying pigs and Hagatha held them in her hands lovingly. Half in jest, she curtsied slightly as she thanked him, extending her shaky hand. Timothy happily continued. "And I have my own set that Mr. B. gave me to open the store on weekends. Don't worry Mrs. B., I'll take good care of your store and keep it organized and clean. I won't lose the keys," he promised. "By the way, I've been keeping an eye on the younger kids when school lets out, just as you said to do." Hagatha smiled, feeling satisfied that everyone's awareness about children's safety was greater because of her efforts, and especially Marcel's; he had sent letters year after year to the schools. Finally, they got the response they had hoped for.

****

Hagatha hugged Sam, letting her mind drift as she looked up above at the angels, the peaceful figures she adored the most. Marcel had promised her he would keep the angels after Christmas as the store's signature. She was relieved that they would be there every day; they gave the entire space a sense of peace and she knew that Clover would have wanted the angels there guiding her. Hagatha's expression was so intent it looked as though the angels were speaking to her.

Timothy followed her and said, "My sister and I are looking forward to working with you and Sam, but there's an important question I have to ask you." Hagatha waited for him to pose his question, all the while looking above her.

"Oh, I'm sure you'll do well in the store," she told him.

"No, Mrs. B., I have another question."

"Oh, I'm sorry, dear." She stood still, then turned and looked into Timothy's eyes and said, "Please ask me. I'm listening."

"Would you mind if we continued calling you 'Haggy' . . . the way we did at school?" he said.

"Oh my! Of course you can!" Hagatha replied. "Everyone can call me Haggy, but would you leave off the 'Baggy' part, please?"

"Yes, of course we will, Mrs. B., I should've made that clear. Most of us never called you that." Timothy smiled at Haggy with a smile that extended from ear to ear. Both of them broke out in laughter.

"But now I have a question for you," she said

with a quasi-serious expression, her eyebrows drawn together. "May I call you Tim and your sister, Meg?"

"Yes, of course you can!" exclaimed Timothy excitedly. "That's what our parents and friends call us." He was so grateful he gave her a hug and she warmly hugged him back. "Haggy it is!" he said. "And Baggy it's not," Hagatha added.

"You know," Hagatha replied, "Haggy used to be my nickname when I was in junior high and high school."

"Really, Mrs. B.?" Tim asked.

"Yes, it's true."

Hagatha's sense of humor showed sparks of returning, and was improving all the time. The first laughs were to be followed by many more.

Hagatha's mother couldn't get enough time with her daughter. She was happy just to be near her even if they weren't speaking every moment. The mere presence of Hagatha satisfied her, especially after thinking for so long that she'd lost both Clover and her daughter. Hagatha's mother felt the closeness they'd always shared, and planned on staying with her for several months. Her dad hugged her every chance he could, and commented to Marcel that his heart was full of happiness and love for his daughter.

The Baggard home was alive and bustling with activity for Christmas Eve. The trimming of their tree with Clover's ornaments had been a great surprise for Hagatha. She told her family she intended to keep the tree up at least two months longer than usual to be reminded of the beauty and significance of family and friends. Each ornament that hung on the green branches of the tree reminded her of Clover.

Christmas dinner was a wonderful adventure for the two mothers and Evelyn—planning, cooking, and baking their recipes alongside one another in the kitchen. Marcel's mother was as good as any professional chef. Everyone was anticipating her expert French cuisine, made with butter and rich sauces. Hagatha's mother made the traditional dishes that comforted her daughter, and Evelyn cooked her creative nouveau mixed cuisine. Loralee tried her hand at making apple pies.

The principal of the Robert Lewis School sent a letter by way of a student to the Baggards. Hagatha asked Timothy to open the envelope that was delivered and to read it out loud to her. "Okay, sure thing," he replied. He read only portions of the letter, parts that, in his judgment, were all she needed to know at the moment. He read:

Dear Mrs. Baggard,
This may be too soon to ask, however, we have a safety curriculum we would like you to teach. It was your perseverance that led us to create this new curriculum. Our staff is awaiting your decision and hopefully you will begin after the New Year, mid-January or February first. We are looking forward to your return to teaching. A later start date would be just fine too if you need more

time . . .

Timothy looked down, then back up at her. Once again, Hagatha had a puzzled look on her face and didn't know what to think. She looked back at him, bewildered. He continued:

> It's called "Clover's Class," a course that teaches children how to be safe when they encounter strangers. It will be a guide for students using the internet and will be mandatory for all grades. There is something special we have to show to you when you come back to school!
> Sincerely,
> George Walker, Principal

Timothy paused for several moments, expecting her to question him about the abruptness of the letter, but her teary eyes were glazed and it appeared as though she was overcome by emotion. He continued reading silently and learned what the special thing was, and decided to keep it as a surprise for Haggy! He knew that the principal would be showing her the plaque commemorating Clover, and her poems and artwork on display in the school hallway, along with the photographs of missing and found children and everyone's else's artwork too— and the written stories in the tall glass shadowbox on the tribute wall.

"That will certainly be another surprise for Haggy," Timothy thought, "but now isn't the time for telling her more."

It was apparent that Hagatha had reached the point where she couldn't concentrate and didn't grasp what she heard—she was excited, perhaps too excited. Her fear of teaching again was overwhelming, and she was speechless as she waited for Timothy to finish reading. Instead of continuing, he folded the letter and told her he would put it in her desk drawer for her to read later on.

"Is that all?" she asked, her voice cracking.

"It's signed by the principal," Timothy told her. "Remember? I read his name to you."

"Yes, you did." Hagatha seemed satisfied. Although she wasn't ready to respond to the principal's note, for the first time in many years she envisioned her own future as something she could actually look forward to. "I just need more time," she said, "just a bit more time." She was anxious, like a child looking forward to the first day of school. Although Timothy was young, he was old enough and bright enough to sense her apprehensions, despite her view of a brighter future, about returning to the classroom.

"Yes, Mrs. B., I totally understand. And I'm sure the school will too."

"Tim, I'm a bit thirsty. Would you please bring me some water?"

"Yes Ma'am, sure thing."

"Tim, you can toss the formal titles out. Just say Haggy."

Marcel walked in and came to Hagatha's side as

Timothy was on his way out of the room. "I'll be right back Mrs. B., umm, I mean, Haggy." Marcel asked, "Is everything okay?"

"Yes Sir. I'm just getting some water for Mrs. B. I mean, Haggy."

"That's all right, Tim," she said. "Haggy, Mrs. B., both are fine."

"Are you feeling all right?" Marcel asked.

Hagatha nodded, but looked somewhat confused. Marcel spoke as he took his wife's arm, to keep her close and calm.

"One step at a time, my dear. Take one step at a time. Evelyn reminded me that Clover's birthday and the birthdays of Timothy and Megan are on the same day, so I was thinking we could celebrate them all together on Christmas with both families! What do you think?" Sam barked as if in agreement.

Hagatha hugged Marcel, and as she kissed Sam on his forehead she said, "I knew that Tim was special in some way when I first met him at school, in the playground, as if he and his sister were sent by my angel."

"It certainly is a strange coincidence that the twins' birthday is the same as Clover's; my heart beat faster the day Megan mentioned that they would be fifteen on the fifteenth of December. I thought that there may be a connection between Clover and the twins."

"Yes Marcel, the same thought occurred to me."

Marcel was delighted that everything was going smoothly. Hagatha was getting back on track. He knew Hagatha would teach again in her own time, however, he was waiting for her strength and confidence to come back first, for her to be the happy soul she used to be—a warm, funny, helpful woman who always attracted others to her. To Marcel, his precious daughter and his wife were still missing. Although he was impatient for his wife to be the way she used to be, he possessed faith that those parts of Hagatha's personality would return fully with each passing day; if not all of her personality then at least some.

"As long as she's with me," he thought, "I don't even care." His mother told him he shouldn't become overly anxious and to be patient with his wife. Marcel could hardly wait to move back home full time. The family and neighbors urged him to take walks during the day, not only to calm himself, but also to give Hagatha some space because she'd been living by herself for so long. "They're right," he thought. "It took years for her to become this way and it may take a year or more to bring her fully back." When Evelyn saw Marcel grinding his jaw, she would take his hand in hers and talk to him to let him know he wasn't alone. "Thanks, Ev," he said, "you and Robert have been the best of friends. I couldn't have done it without you."

Timothy assured Mr. B. he could learn how to paint furniture and do errands. Marcel arranged for Timothy and Megan to stop by the house on their days off once he went back to work. "I'll teach you how to paint and stain," he told them. Their neighbors discussed what they could do to help Hagatha's recovery along, and agreed to take turns making lunch for Hagatha as well as dinner if needed, and asked Marcel to let them know if he'd be working late. Megan baked oatmeal raisin cookies as treats for Hagatha and brought them to her at least once a week; and Hagatha raved about how good they tasted, like cookies a professional baker would make but even better because they were homemade.

"Why don't we package them with ribbons and tags to sell in the store?" Hagatha asked.

Megan was thrilled! It was her own recipe—a little taken from Martha Stewart and a little from her grandmother's recipe. Brown sugar was the secret ingredient.

Megan said, "I'm going to try my hand at baking cakes next."

"I'm sure you'll be great at it," Hagatha replied. "But take your time. There's only enough room in the store for your cookies. We'll put them by the register."

Hagatha's mom told her that the neighbors were wonderful and had offered to give her whatever help she needed, day or night. She responded with gratitude and was touched by their desire to make her life as easy as possible as she recovered. Her mom also said that she intended to visit Hagatha during the next year until she was settled and felt better. "Evelyn will stop by to see you every evening after her family finishes dinner," her dad told her.

Loralee wanted to spend her spare time with Hagatha and visited her often, knowing that Christmas vacation would soon be over and she wouldn't be seeing her until spring break. Marcel appreciated her generosity with her time and expressed his heartfelt thanks to both Evelyn and Loralee many times over.

The warmth of the Baggard's home and Clover's spiritual presence was evident in the many gestures of kindness made by everyone. Marcel brought his wife a dozen roses for their dining room table just as he did on every birthday, Christmas, and Valentine's Day. For Valentine's Day, the roses were always pink for her and pink clover for Clover; on Christmas the roses were American Beauty red. The florist was happy to see Marcel again and gave him an extra dozen roses as a gift to welcome Hagatha back. Marcel placed the extra ones in their bedroom, between two wingback chairs, on the table with the reading lamp he and Hagatha bought on the Cape. The roses gave the bedroom a sense of life and a romantic ambiance. He took one red rose and one pink rose to put on Clover's night table, adding to the pink assortment Loralee and Evelyn had left. Hagatha watched Marcel put the pink rose on Clover's dresser in her favorite pink vintage vase. The moment was special, and Sam underscored its significance by jumping up on Clover's bed, barking and wagging his tail for playtime. Hagatha was amused and a smile lit up her face. Marcel turned to her and winked as Sam romped and played.

The holiday china was set out, with the crystal water glasses they used only for New Year's Eve parties. The glasses glistened and sparkled, reflecting off the chandelier hanging above them. The hallway walls were covered with photographs of good memories from the past; Marcel's mother had decorated for days. There were china figures of Santa and his reindeers displayed on the fireplace ledge along with beautifully painted figurines. The relatives who had gone home called almost daily, while those who stayed for Christmas and New Year's blessed the Baggards with even greater joy. Hagatha's mother stayed close by her side—and it was a comfort. They would sit together in Clover's room for short periods of time talking, not wanting to linger there too long, then move around the house room to room, talking and reminiscing.

Clover's bedroom door was left ajar, open just as if she were there. Marcel's father sat in Clover's room looking through her decorating books, with Sam lying beside him chewing on one of his new toys.

Marcel happened to go by Clover's room at 6 a.m., and caught his father reading her books aloud as he did when Clover was a child. Clover's presence occupied the room, and everyone who entered felt it.

Sometimes, Hagatha came into the room with Marcel and they leaned back against the many pillows, daydreaming and hugging one another from time to time. On a few occasions they even fell asleep there. Christmas and the long-awaited birthday celebration arrived. Not only were they celebrating the anniversary of Clover's birthday, but Timothy and Megan's birthdays as well. There was an enormous combination Christmas and birthday cake that was made by their favorite bakery for everyone to share. The frosting was chocolate, decorated with pink fairies and clover. It was put in the barn where customers and friends could mull around while shopping for items and help themselves to small pieces of cake pre-cut for them, various juices, hot tea, and Marcel's imported coffee.

Hagatha was looking at her home with all its treasures, arranging them the same way she did long ago. The house was different but it was alive, animated by the high spirits of the people within. Everyone put on their coats and headed outside for the short trek to Haggy B's.

Hagatha felt ready as she took Marcel's hand, with Sam following behind. Marcel was wearing the red wool sweater his mother started knitting for him in France and finished during the evenings after dinner. She would sit for hours so that he would be able to wear it for Christmas Eve and Christmas Day. She made Hagatha a beautiful red scarf with pink crocheted clover on the side, using six of Clover's pink vintage buttons. "You look absolutely gorgeous!" Marcel told her. Her new dress, which his mother had bought for her, looked amazing with her smooth, rosy complexion and beautiful smile that shone with a radiance Marcel hadn't seen in years. Hagatha felt proud of herself. Clover was there with them at the house and with every step they took to the barn. There were so many people gathered together in Haggy B's. When Marcel walked in with Hagatha, his face showed the same happiness he once felt on their first date and on the day they were married.

Hagatha's personality was vibrant, and she was healthier now with the few pounds that sat on her bones from eating heaps of holiday food. Her hair had become silky and bounced with each step she took, the few strands of gray blending in with her blonde highlights to give her a dignified appearance.

Timothy and Megan watched as Marcel took a pair of scissors and cut the red Christmas ribbon that stretched across the brass register. Flowers filled the barn, sent by friends and from people the Baggards didn't even know. One big bunch of pink and white roses was sent by the men's shelter. Now the barn was officially open for business! The party was about to begin and Hagatha blushed with excitement. Marcel toasted the birthdays of Clover, Tim, and Megan, and wished them well on this day of celebration.

The time had come for Hagatha to accept and move beyond her profound loss. Loralee carried the stuffed dog Sammy to the barn. Sam growled at the toy thinking it could be another animal, but Loralee calmed him down right away saying, "Sammy, it's stuffed, not real," and he wagged his tail exuberantly. She called the toy her "lucky Clover piece."

While they were celebrating, Loralee stood close

to Hagatha, who sensed her warmth and felt more secure. She hugged Loralee, and Loralee told her that she would be glad to go with her to find old furniture for the store when she came home for the break in March.

"That is," she said, "if it's all right with you . . . "

The answer was "Yes, of course, I'll always welcome your company!" Hagatha and Loralee had become so close it was as if Clover's presence were there in the barn for Hagatha as well as for Loralee. Loralee always said Hagatha was her second mom, and Hagatha said that her closeness to Loralee made her feel as though she had another daughter.

Sam barked at the people as he stumbled about looking for crumbs to eat—a real moocher. He barked at the angels hanging down from the ceiling, tethered by invisible strings and floating tranquilly above them.

Marcel looked up. Hagatha lifted her gaze to join his and said, "Clover's presence is here in the barn. Heaven is in our barn."

"Yes, my dear Hagatha—it is."

Loralee glanced at the desk where she had put a gift wrapped in shiny paper and marked for Hagatha. She gave it to her. "This is for you," Loralee said.

"Goodness my dear, is it from you?" Hagatha asked.

"Oh no. It's not my gift, but I do know who it's from."

Opening the bag, she read a card that said "BELIEVE" in bold print, and underneath read,

"When you believe in your dreams, whether big or small, near or far, they will come true." The signature was "From a mother who believed."

Hagatha experienced an initial rush of energy as she held the card in her hand. Loralee told her it was from the mother whose missing daughter was eventually found and reunited with her family after years of searching. Hagatha hugged Loralee. "I will cherish this gift always. I would've liked to meet this woman," Hagatha said somewhat disappointedly. Loralee explained that the woman had said she would be away for the holidays and regretted that she couldn't give Hagatha her gift in person. "Perhaps we'll meet someday," Hagatha said with a sigh.

The celebration marked the Baggards' reconciliation as a couple. They were finally back together and their marriage was on the way to being restored. With his brother's help, Marcel brought all his clothes and personal belongings back to his home; together, they talked and kept Clover's memory alive inside their hearts.

When the holidays were over, Hagatha decided to teach Clover's class at the Robert Lewis Elementary School—as much to keep Clover's memory alive as to resume teaching for the sake of her sanity. She needed to feel useful and to know that her life had meaning. Plans were underway for Hagatha to have her own classroom, where her students would come to discuss practical safety measures they could take in order to prevent a tragedy such as Clover's.

Marcel continued with his own work on ways to protect children from online predators. He started another website, this time with a blog to help others with support and funds.

When Hagatha and Marcel made a visit to the school to see her new classroom, Marcel and Principal Walker showed her the plaque dedicated to Clover and the amazing tribute wall. The shadowbox containing the children's stories moved her to such a degree that they asked the principal's secretary for a copy of each one to take home with them.

Hagatha was so apprehensive on her first day back in the classroom that one student had to bring her orange juice from the cafeteria because she thought she was going to faint!

Timothy left the principal's letter where Hagatha could easily find it, and eventually she read the letter he had written to her about Clover's class. She realized that Timothy hadn't read the entire letter to her to protect her from feeling overwhelmed, but now she was ready to take on the children, parents, and school with a renewed sense of herself and her own importance, and she busied herself with projects that held meaning for her. Hagatha sent a handmade card to each of the students who would be taking her class, personally welcoming them to her classroom. Hagatha's mother visited every other month and stayed with her for a week at a time. Hagatha was on a smooth upward trajectory. She took care of her appearance and her mind. At school, the young bullies who had taunted Hagatha were stunned by her transformation, and in turn, they changed. They had listened to her and were not the same on account of her—to the amazement of their teachers. Her influence transformed their anger into positive energy.

Finally, Hagatha had succeeded in gathering enough strength to accept that her daughter was gone, and despite that, she was still happy. She found peace. Like Marcel, Hagatha hoped that Clover might be out there somewhere trying to come back home. They would never stop looking and believing.

Detectives and police were still searching; her file remained open. A picture of Clover's face was reposted on buildings and online. The window shade in Clover's room was kept up even on rainy or cold winter days. The ritual of closing the shades, like the times Hagatha would shut down, were over. She would always clean Clover's room, making sure to fluff the pillows on her bed.

If she felt a moment of despair, she shared it immediately with Marcel or her parents—or Evelyn, who was her confidante. When she experienced sadness, Hagatha would sit with Marcel in her bedroom nook, Sam beside them, gazing at the fresh tulips Marcel brought home every week. When a cool breeze passed by them in the silence of the evening, sometimes, they thought, it was a message from Clover. As Hagatha accepted her sadness as part of her life, the more cheerful she became helping her students. It was truly the beginning of a new life for her.

Timothy and Megan became like part of the family, and all the people in town were happy to have Hagatha and Haggy B's Barn back. Hagatha finally read all the letters she had received over the years, and painstakingly responded to each one of them. Marcel repeatedly vowed never to leave her side again, and even when he lived away from her, he told her, he maintained his faith that she would one day recover. Friends and family had lifted their spirits and helped bring them to this point of serenity.

CHAPTER 15

HELLO!

Life for the Baggards proceeded according to plan. With the help of the police, Hagatha and Marcel devised a curriculum for the safety of both younger and older children outside of school and on the internet. Marcel's website, "Clover's Club," was popular—a "go to" source for parents, teachers, and young people. Parents of the children in their town wholeheartedly supported the efforts of the Baggards, and the schools implemented the courses with Hagatha as lead teacher. The classes were held every week for six weeks, which gave her time to work in the store with Timothy, who had become quite expert at woodworking.

****

It was not long before Hagatha was bustling—rearranging furniture and taking care of customers. The weeks were passing by like fast-moving clouds

271

in the sky. She was always aware of the presence of the angels floating above her in the rafters. Sam was growing in leaps and bounds and became larger than either Marcel or Hagatha ever imagined.

As soon as customers entered the barn, she would help them by suggesting certain items according to her sense of what they would like. "Welcome to Haggy B's and Clover's Angel Barn," she would say as Sam barked. Marcel's work schedule prevented him from helping out during the day, but he hurried home after work like a smitten schoolboy. Every night Hagatha had dinner waiting for him, and a place for Clover was set at the table without fail for their peace of mind.

Timothy and Megan proved to be invaluable, keeping the items in the store dusted and organized. In addition to making her exquisite oatmeal raisin cookies to sell at the store, Megan, as it turned out, was an adept salesgirl and Timothy proved to be a fledgling accountant, keeping track of the inventory and sales. Hagatha scouted for old furniture she could refinish, sometimes with Loralee on Sunday afternoons when she spent the weekend home instead of at school.

Sam was there with Hagatha every step of the way, like her shadow, and most often he was underfoot with his gangling, growing legs. She bought an old red wagon from a yard sale and refinished it so Sam, fitted with a padded harness, could pull it just as Clover envisioned years ago. A salvaged upholstered cushion served him well in his bed, which was still next to the register. Sales were brisk, and although the pace could be tiring, the more Hagatha did, the greater energy she had, and she embraced her new life with zest. Time flew by . . .

The transformation Marcel hoped for all those years came true. Hagatha was her old self— energetic, ready with a smile and sweet words of encouragement for everyone.

Marcel and Hagatha were as close as they used to be, perhaps even more connected as a result of losing their only daughter and their lengthy journey back from that. In the spring and summer, they picnicked next to the lake together every chance they got. Marcel now was certain that for their marriage to thrive Hagatha had to have her own space and time when necessary. His sense of what to do turned out to be the wisest way of dealing with his wife's deep-rooted sorrow. The process had taken years, and might have taken even longer had they intervened with doctors and pills. Now they had each other to rely on whenever either of them had a bad day; and those days became fewer and farther between.

Teaching the safety class together lifted their spirits. The customers kept Hagatha busy buying used items and having her re-do them over and over. Tim and Megan celebrated several birthdays in the old barn and could run the barn without any help when the Baggards took time to get away, which wasn't often. Hagatha and Marcel's belief in Clover's return never wavered.

Another three years had passed and the holidays were once again upon them. It was two days before Christmas. Everything was going along just fine. Timothy and Megan's birthday party was a more lavish affair than ever before because they would be graduating from high school. They were using their time off to work at the store before they started business school next September. Timothy wasn't entirely sure what his major would be, but he let Hagatha know that he'd do her taxes for her because he most probably would concentrate his studies in accounting. He had also acquired a collection of vintage toys and comics that pleased Hagatha no end. One afternoon, when Hagatha was helping a customer with holiday decorations in the barn, the phone rang. She and Timothy were in the store, and rather than excusing herself for a moment, he went to answer as he always did. Sam, as usual, was underfoot and Timothy tripped over him, fumbling for the receiver.

"Be cool, Sam boy," he said. "Gotta answer the phone." Finally, he managed to pick up the receiver and say hello. The voice at the other end must have said something disturbing because Timothy turned pale and could barely breathe as he tried to swallow the hard lump in his throat. He couldn't speak. Gesturing to Hagatha, he indicated that the call was for her as he lay the receiver down on the desk. Seeing that Timothy looked pallid and was in distress, she rushed over and, standing by his side, placed a hand on his arm to steady him.

"Are you okay?" she asked. He pointed to the receiver for her to pick it up. She couldn't imagine what was wrong with Timothy. For a moment she was afraid it was her mother on the phone and something awful had happened to her dad.

"Good afternoon, Haggy B's," she managed to say with her smiley and cheerful voice. There was silence at the other end, a pregnant pause . . .

And the next words she heard were a teary, "Hello, Mom?"

Hagatha's heart skipped a beat and her knees buckled beneath her as she fell to the floor.

"Hello? Mom?"

The belief the Baggards had in Clover's return had been answered by the reality of Clover's questioning voice at the other end of the phone. It was a triumph of the human spirit over adversity as much as it was miraculous, both for the Baggards and Clover. Timothy rushed to Hagatha's side.

"Clover? Clover!" Hagatha shouted into the phone. "Oh my baby, it's you!"

Yes, there are such things as miracles!

The Baggards' Christmas will be celebrated with the greatest joy imaginable this year.

Happy Holidays to All!

Always Believe!

Best holiday wishes from Hagatha,
Marcel, Sam the dog, Loralee,
Evelyn, Richard,
Timothy and Megan, all the children from school,
and their special Christmas gift,
Clover!

The End

ABOUT THE AUTHOR

Libbe Leah, born and raised in Boston, is the author of books for both children and adults. She also collects and repurposes antiques, and has a great passion for real estate, especially old homes, which she reinvigorates with her knowledge of restoration and eye for décor. She has done public speaking at such places as Mass Mental Health Services, and participated in a seminar for doctors and nurses about death and dying at the JFK Presidential Library. Although not a licensed practitioner, Libbe is nonetheless a gifted counselor, helping those in need with understanding and often sage advice. In addition to this book, many more novels and a memoir are forthcoming.

Made in the USA
Columbia, SC
27 August 2018